The Beach House Mystery

Samantha Wolf Mysteries

#3

TARA ELLIS

ISBN-13: 978-1515141877
ISBN-10: 151514187X

The Beach House Mystery

When I first sat down to brainstorm the next adventure for Sam and Ally; all I knew was that it would happen during the last part of their summer break. Like so many other authors, I once again drew from some of my own experiences to conjure up a story. The coast of Washington State and Oregon hold some very special memories for me. As a child, my family would often travel there over the summer, and as always, my best friend Lisa would come along! We might not have dug up quite the same level of mysteries that Sam and Ally manage, but we always had fun trying. Once I decided on the setting, it was a fun challenge to imagine all of the things that would make this a true seafaring tale! I hope that you enjoy this installment as much I have while writing it.

A special thanks (as always!) to my ever-faithful BETA readers: Lisa Hansen, Cindy Pierce, and my biggest fan and mom, Linda Morris!!

Samantha Wolf Mysteries

1. The Mystery of Hollow Inn
2. The Secret of Camp Whispering Pines
3. The Beach House Mystery
4. The Heiress of Covington Ranch
5. The Haunting of Eagle Creek Middle School
6. A Mysterious Christmas on Orcas Island

Find these and Tara's other titles on her author page!

http://www.amazon.com/author/taraellis

CONTENTS

1

A LATE SUMMER SURPRISE

Sam would have *never* guessed what her next adventure was going to be, even if given the chance to dream one up. Sitting at the dinner table with her two-year-old twin sisters to one side, and her older fourteen-year-old brother on the other, she's completely unsuspecting of the grin her father has on his face when he sits down.

Her mom passes the roast to him without comment, but Sam notices the look that they exchange. Pausing with the fork halfway to her mouth, she sets it back on the plate and crosses her arms.

"Okay, what's up?" she asks cautiously, raising her eyebrows when her dad tries to act innocent.

"Why do you ask?" he says coyly, while making a mountain out of his mashed potatoes.

"Come on, Dad," Sam insists. "You know you're no good at lying. I can see *right* through you!"

Curious now, her brother Hunter breaks away from devouring everything on his plate. Narrowing his eyes, he stares first at his dad, and then their mom. Looking approvingly at Sam, he is apparently impressed with her observation skills. "Definitely hiding something," he mumbles, nodding vigorously, his mouth still full of food.

Butterflies suddenly come to life in Sam's stomach as her hopes swell over whatever the obvious surprise is. She's been begging for a horse of her own for years, so that's her first thought. The old, empty barn in the far corner of their three-acre property is the perfect spot for one. The money and time that her parents insist are lacking is the only hang-up.

The fluttering settles almost as fast as it

began though, when Sam quickly realizes how unlikely it is. Her mom and dad were talking last night about how tight money is again this month. Sam also recently had her twelfth birthday, a few months ago, so any chance of a horse is probably a good year away still. But what could it be?

"Don't talk with your mouth full, Hunter," their mom scolds. "You're going to choke one of these days."

"Classic distraction tactic," Hunter counters, still chewing.

Grinning now, Kathy Wolf looks to her husband and gives him an obvious wink. "They're onto us, Ethan," she whispers loudly.

"Nothing gets past you, Samantha," Ethan laughs, pushing his full plate to the side and slapping the table with his palms. "I *do* have an announcement!"

Ignoring the use of her formal name, Sam leans forward eagerly. Her dad doesn't usually put on this kind of a show. It must be *good*.

"You know that I was talking about how my boss, Mr. Stiles, was shopping around for a new boat?" Sam and Hunter both nod, while the twins paint their highchairs with gravy.

"Well, he found one, but it needs a lot of work. It's in dry dock in a small town out on the Olympic Peninsula, and he wants me to oversee the job."

Sam's smile wavers as her dad reveals the big news. She doesn't really see how this is supposed to be exciting. He works as a commercial fisherman for several months out of the year up in Alaska, and often does maintenance work for his boss in the off months. Mr. Stiles has several boats, so he has men fishing for him almost year-round. Her dad goes after halibut, and runs a boat from August through November. Since it's now late July, money's getting tight.

So he's going to be in charge of some guys fixing an old boat, Sam thinks to herself. *I guess that means we don't have to worry anymore about money this month.* That's great, of course, but it still doesn't explain why her parents are acting this way.

"That's good news, Dad," Hunter offers. "But what does it have to do with us?"

Sam glances at her brother, relieved that she's not the only one confused, even though he dedicates most of his free time to finding new and creative ways to drive her crazy.

"Because Mr. Stiles has offered your dad the use of his vacation cabin on the beach, while he's there in Wood's Cove!" Kathy interjects, clapping her hands. The twins pick up on their mom's excitement and begin clapping their hands too, squealing in delight.

Shushing the two little girls, Ethan tries to explain. "The cabin has four bedrooms, and is located *right* on the beach in the cove. He's given me permission to use it for as long as I'm there, and I can bring whoever I want."

"The town, Wood's Cove," Sam's mom continues, "is a neat little tourist spot. They have all sorts of activities on the private beach. I think you kids would just *love* it!"

"Four bedrooms?" Sam questions, her hopes rising. The fluttering has returned, as she realizes the potential for something great, after all.

"Yes," Ethan confirms. "Plenty of room for all of us...plus you and Hunter can each bring a friend."

Jumping up from her chair, Sam almost knocks it over in her excitement. Everyone already knows she'll bring her best friend, Ally. The two have been inseparable for years. They've already solved two mysteries this summer, although both could have ended badly. Fortunately, no one was hurt, but her parents have kept a very tight leash on her for the past few weeks, as a result.

"We figure the best way to keep an eye on you and Ally is to have you with us," Kathy states while looking closely at her daughter. The message is clear.

Sitting back down slowly, Sam tries to contain her emotions. Her parents had thought that she and Ally would stay out of trouble at summer camp, but *trouble* seems to have a way of finding *them*. Although nothing that happened on their other adventures was really their fault, they've earned a reputation. Sam knows that if her parents were able to see the escapades she was already dreaming up for the beach…they might just change their minds.

"Oh, I know, Mom!" she agrees. "I'm sure we'll spend most of our time on the beach by the house, and of course we'll help watch the twins!"

Sam watches her mother squint her eyes

suspiciously and study her. While Sam's tall for her age, she's not too slim, but rather sturdy. Her long brown hair is pulled back out of the way, as usual. A nice row of freckles, brought out by the summer sun, dance up and down as she crinkles her nose at her mother. "What?" she asks, innocently.

"You know *what*," Hunter interrupts. "You're totally going to get into trouble somehow. Probably get us all arrested, and make dad lose his job."

Mustering up the dirtiest look she can, Sam crosses her arms and bites her bottom lip in response. She knows better than to get into an argument with him.

"That's enough," Ethan reprimands, effectively ending the confrontation. "I think even *Sam* would have a hard time finding mischief at Wood's Cove," he adds good-naturedly. Turning his attention to Hunter, he asks, "Are you going to ask Jeff to come?"

Distracted by the question, Hunter turns from Sam to his father. "Nah...he's still in New York with his parents, at his sister's wedding. They won't be back for more than a week. When are we going?"

"Two days. We leave early Monday morning," Ethan says, eying his son closely. He knows that Jeff is his only close friend anymore.

"Why don't you ask John?"

"Humph!" Hunter snorts, rolling his eyes for extra emphasis. "Are you kidding, Dad? I'm sure he's got football practice, or numerous dates lined up."

Kathy's brows furrow at her son's sarcasm, but she refrains from commenting on it. John is Ally's older brother, and it's a touchy subject.

Sam briefly considers blurting out a smart comeback that floats through her head, but holds back. Hunter might not be that nice to her, but they used to be very close when they were younger. They're only two years apart, and Sam can still remember following him around everywhere, copying everything he did, until he wouldn't tolerate it. That occurred when Hunter started middle school, which Sam is about to do this school year. She kind of understands now how much pressure he was feeling to fit in. It was then that he and John drifted apart, too, because John started high school. He's still a nice guy and all, but he's got a different schedule, friends, and sports.

It was a year of change, with her mom having the twins and quitting her job as a teacher to stay home. That in turn caused the money issues, but it never really seemed to put much of a damper on things. They always get by somehow.

Hunter appears to be rethinking his dad's suggestion, running both of his hands through his thick, dark hair in a gesture that Sam has come to recognize as one that he makes when deep in thought. They both inherited their father's dark features, but Sam scored on the height gene, while Hunter seems destined to dwell on the short end of the spectrum with his mother. The twins sport the same blonde, naturally curly hair as their mom.

"I guess it might not hurt to ask," Hunter finally agrees before diving back into his food. This surprises Sam.

"Great!" Kathy says happily, while trying to mop up the gravy from the high chairs before it spills onto the floor. "I'll call over and talk with their mom tonight. I know that she'll expect the invitation to come from us, as parents. They're a bit more formal that way."

Her appetite gone, replaced with a sense of anticipation, Sam tries to picture the beach house and what the cove might look like. The small town they live in is located in the northwestern part of Washington State, right next to the ocean. But the area south of them, out on the majestic, rain-forested Olympic Peninsula, is much different than home. Picturing craggy cliffs, mysterious woods and sunken treasure, Sam knows she isn't going to sleep much until Monday.

2

FINDING THE COVE

The red van pulls away from Sam's house right on schedule, early Monday morning. Ordered to sit in the dreaded space located at the back of the van, in between the twin's car seats, Sam is doing her best to remain optimistic.

Looking at the back of Ally's head, covered in vibrant red hair, she focuses on the destination, rather than the journey. Their older brothers are seated to either side of her best friend, and based on the locker-room smell that is already starting to permeate the vehicle, Sam decides that maybe she *didn't* get the worst spot.

Twisting around on the bench seat, as if

reading her mind, Ally peers over the headrest and squints at Sam. "My eyes are burning," she gasps, making guppy motions with her lips. "Help me!"

Laughing now, her torment from just moments ago already forgotten, Sam scoots as far forward as her seatbelt will allow. "I've got one word of advice for you guys," she says to John and Hunter, who are now lifting their arms over Ally's ducked head. "Deodorant."

"Where's the fun in *that?*" Hunter responds, but lowers his arm when it appears that Ally might actually be gagging. Ally's brother has no pity though. John continues to keep his arm draped across the back of the seat, smiling at Hunter in camaraderie. With his blonde hair and tall stature, you would never guess that he and Ally were siblings, if it weren't for the same intense, blue eyes.

It's good to see them getting along so well, Sam thinks to herself, even if it's at the expense of her friend's stomach. Both she and Hunter had been surprised when John called Saturday night. Their mom had just gotten off the phone with Ally's parents, explaining the trip. Sam had assumed it was her best friend phoning to talk about it.

Turns out that John *doesn't* have football this week. To Hunter's astonishment, he accepts the invitation. Although her brother doesn't say much about it, Sam knows that it means a lot to him. He's starting high school this year, and having his old friend to hang out with will be a huge relief.

Doing her best to steady her stomach, Ally holds her breath and elbows John in the ribs, causing her brother to lower his arm. Smiling at his grimace, she refuses to let anything spoil her mood, and happily suggests that they play a game.

The four of them spend the next two hours finding various types of cars, license plates, words on street signs and animals in pastures. It's been quite some time since they've all been together like this, but they fall back into their old habits as if it were just yesterday.

As the van pulls off the main interstate, and onto the highway that will take them into the Olympic Mountains, Sam pauses in their banter to study the rising peaks. Although she's lived near them all her life, she really didn't know much of the history until studying about it last year in school. She actually wrote a paper called, 'The *Other* Mountains in Washington State,' because most people thought that the Cascades were the only noteworthy range.

The Olympics were one of the last wilderness areas in America to be explored, and the area wasn't mapped until nearly 1900. It's basically a big arm of land that sticks out into Puget Sound, with the Pacific Ocean to the west. Its northern point is the farthest in the states. The massive rainforests cover about half of it, and there are tons of state and federal parks that are filled with natural lakes and rivers, teaming with fish. They've been camping there a few times, but this will be the first trip that involves staying on the beach.

Tilting her head, Sam thinks back over the various family vacations and other gatherings they've been to. Nope. Never stayed in any sort of beach house before.

"Come on, Ginger. It's your turn!"

"I've told you before not to call me that!" Ally says loudly, doing her best to give Hunter a dirty look. He has his numerous things to tease the two girls about, and Ally's bright hair is his favorite.

"Shh!" Sam cautions, looking fearfully at the two sleeping twins. Even though their nap guarantees they'll be running around all crazy after they get to the beach house, she doesn't care. The silence in the back of the van for the past hour has been worth it.

"Look down there, kids!" Ethan calls out, unaware of the need to whisper. "You can see the cove from here."

Ignoring the stirring two-year-olds, Sam absently wiggles their binkies back into their mouths while staring out the window. Sure enough, far below them and barely visible through the passing trees is what appears to be a large cove, an inlet of water on the ocean side of the peninsula. The northern end looks to be dotted with houses, while at southern end boasts a large marina, filled with boats.

"Look!" Sam gasps, dropping a binky to point excitedly. "An old lighthouse!"

High cliffs cut a dramatic outline against the ocean, extending out past the homes to the north of the cove. Tapering down to large boulders and an expanse of flat ground, a tall, white lighthouse sits on the farthest point.

Sam moans when it drops out of view and they start to descend into the trees. Her brief delight is rewarded with two crying toddlers. Desperately trying to silence them with various toys and snacks, she misses the sign announcing their arrival to the town.

"We're here!" Kathy announces enthusiastically. "Oh! Look at all of the shops. This is just perfect!"

Craning her neck to try to see around everyone, Sam continues her efforts to calm her little sisters as her dad looks for the realtor's office. They're supposed to pick up the keys to the beach house there. The business is responsible for maintaining the property in the off-season, and sometimes rents it out for Mr. Stiles.

When the van finally comes to a stop, Sam is the first one to fight her way out into the fresh air. Although she doesn't normally get carsick, the cramped, noisy space got to her. Sucking in the cool, salty offshore breeze, Sam closes her eyes and concentrates on the feeling of solid ground.

"Sam!" Ally practically yells. "You *have* to see this." Grabbing her best friend by the arm, Ally drags Sam along the sidewalk. Ignoring the slightly green tinge on Sam's face, Ally turns her so that she's facing an entrance to an outdoor courtyard, lined with quaint stores.

"I don't get it," Sam admits. "I know you like to shop, Ally, but why do *I* have to see it?" Already feeling much better, Sam looks more closely at the nice, wooden boardwalk in the courtyard. It's cute, but not exactly what she would call exciting.

"Not the *stores*, silly!" Ally laughs, and grasps Sam's shoulders. Turning her to the right, she points at a large, wooden statue near them. "That!"

Blinking, Sam tries to figure out what she's looking at. It's a carving depicting something part fish, part shark and part man. It has the body of a fish, but the head and fins of a shark…with very distinct, human looking eyes and arms. Next to it is an ornate, wooden sign that reads "Wood's Sea Creature," with no further explanation.

"Well, that's creepy," John says from

behind Sam. Turning, she sees that all of the kids have gathered on the sidewalk, including her mom with the twins.

Looking back to the 'creature,' Sam manages to hide the growing smile from her mom, but Ally spots it and moves closer. Silently, she puts an arm around her best friend.

"I think we're going to like it here," Ally whispers.

3

THE BEACH HOUSE

Their break is cut short when Ethan returns dangling the keys and orders them all back into the van. Since the whole town is essentially next to the ocean, it only takes a few minutes to reach the beach house. It's located at the end of a wooded, private road, and isn't too impressive from the driveway. But from the water-facing side, its vast rooms, featuring enormous windows, reveal its true size.

The kids all race up the porch and scramble to be the first inside, wanting to get dibs on the best room. As soon as they see the decorations though, it's clear that it isn't going to be an issue.

In the far back corner of the house, there's a large bedroom with two twin beds. The walls are painted various shades of blue and are adorned with everything having to do with boats. The curtains have sailboats on them, the light is a big anchor, and the bedspreads depict various pirate ships. In addition to the boyish décor, there's also a big TV equipped with a gaming system. John and Hunter throw their bags on the floor and start looking at the games piled up in front of it.

Across the hall on the ocean side is an identical space. But when Sam and Ally step into it, they're transported to a very different world. While Sam doesn't normally like girly stuff, she has to admit to herself that the explosion of pastel colors is welcoming. One of the walls is covered with a large mural, depicting the old lighthouse Sam saw on the way in. Soaring seagulls surround it, and water sprays up from waves crashing against jagged rocks beneath it.

The bedding, curtains, throw rugs and pictures all seem to match the colors used in the painting and continue with the ocean theme. The best part, though, are the double glass doors that open onto a private deck overlooking the beach.

"Oh my gosh!" Sam exclaims, holding the doors wide. "Ally, you've *got* to look at this view. This is *so* much better than I thought it would be!"

Coming to stand beside her, Ally links her arm through Sam's. The briny smelling breeze lifts their hair and billows the curtains behind them. Gulls cry out overhead, looking for food. A white-sand beach spreads out below them, meeting up with the ocean not more than a few hundred feet away. Surprisingly, there are only a few people visible on the open stretch, giving them a sense of privacy.

Far off to the right, the pictured lighthouse rises up impressively from the peninsula that ends in a sharp cliff-face. Thick evergreens spread out to either side and reach more than halfway out on the spit of land, before giving in to the rocky, windblown surface.

Turning to look more closely for neighboring houses, Sam can just barely make out a white clapboard structure through the woods on their left. It appears that they truly are the last place on the block, though, reaffirming the feeling of isolation.

The hairs on the back of her neck rising due to more than the brisk wind, Sam finally looks at Ally. She finds that her friend is already staring at her with a knowing, telltale grin on her freckled face.

"Sam…" Ally says cautiously. "We *can't* get into any trouble while we're here!"

Giving her arm a reassuring squeeze, Sam turns back to the ocean. "How could we possibly get into trouble? I'm just thinking how much fun it's going to be to go exploring. Look at this place!"

Pulling her smart phone out of her back pocket, Ally holds out her prized possession to take a picture. Turning it around, she tugs Sam towards her for a selfie. Lining it up so that the lighthouse peaks out from in between their heads, she takes several shots until the angle is just right.

Tapping her foot impatiently while waiting to get Ally's attention again, Sam watches as she attempts the sharing and uploading process.

"*Why* am I not surprised?" Ally finally says

in disgust, jamming the phone back into her pocket.

"No service?" Sam guesses, trying to hide a smile. She couldn't care less if they're 'connected' or not. She had only just gotten her first phone a few months ago, for her twelfth birthday. Their trip to Montana earlier in the summer had been the first time in a *long* time that Ally had gone without constant cell access. It turned out to be a good thing, though. It gave them the chance to get back to the basics of what had made them such good friends in the first place.

At the summer camp they went to recently, the phones hadn't been allowed. So while Sam suspects Ally will make a big stink about it, she also knows that her friend will do just fine without it.

"There's one bar of phone service," Ally replies, leaning on the weather-beaten bannister. "But it's not letting me connect to the internet." Shrugging, she squints up at the summer sun high overhead. "Do you think we could go swimming?"

"Sam! Hunter!" Sam's mom starts calling

for them, and she raises her eyebrows at Ally.

"I have a feeling we'll have to do a few other things *first*," she tells her friend. "But it's barely noon. Plenty of time!"

Linking arms again, they make their way back out to the kitchen, where everyone is gathering. The twins apparently found a room well suited for them, too. They both have toys in each hand that Sam has never seen before.

"Ball!" Tabitha shouts, holding it out to show everyone. They refer to her as the oldest, since she was born twenty minutes before her sister. Thankfully, her hair is growing much faster for some reason, making it easier to tell them apart.

"*My* ball!" Addison cries, dropping her own loot so she can try to take it. This leads to a screaming match, and then to both of them sitting on the floor crying, when Kathy takes the ball away.

"Time for lunch?" Ethan asks his wife, plugging his ears.

Nodding, Kathy takes the car keys from him in exchange for the ball, and gestures to the kids. "They're all yours. I'm going back into town to get some grocery shopping done. Sam," she adds, turning to the two girls. "Please help with the twins until I get back. After we all eat, you guys can go explore the beach."

Meanwhile, John and Hunter have been slowly making their way back towards the hall...and escape. "Hold up boys!" Kathy calls. "Don't think I forgot about you."

Groaning, Hunter drags his feet dramatically the few steps back. "Sam's practically been gone all summer," he nearly whines. "I've been stuck at home with the super duo."

Crossing her arms in an 'I'm not falling for that' stance, Kathy tilts her head in his direction. "Oh really? Because that's not quite how I remember it. Seems to me you've spent just about every minute this summer doing exactly what you wanted. The only time you sat for the twins, was when Sam traded you for it. I expect you to do your fair share of helping this week. Understood?"

"It's okay, Mom," Sam interjects, before Hunter has a chance to weigh in. "I know I've gotten to do a lot this summer, and I really don't mind playing with them."

The room is silent for a minute, as even the twins seem surprised by their sister's generosity. But they break the spell by giggling over a spinning gadget, their earlier fight already forgotten.

Eying her daughter suspiciously, Kathy hesitates. "Okay…I guess you two can start your free time now," she finally says to John and Hunter. Looking back at Sam, her eyebrows furrow. The boys join Kathy in staring suspiciously at Sam, but then quickly run off before anyone has a change of heart.

"What?" Sam finally blurts out when even Ally acts confused. "I'd rather just play with Tabitha and Addison by ourselves, is all. The boys will just tease us and make them cry. It's easier this way."

Apparently convinced, Kathy shrugs and then blows her husband a kiss. When the front door closes behind her, Ethan settles his own questioning gaze on Sam.

"Remember," he warns. "No funny business while we're here." Not looking for a response, he picks up the remaining bags from the front hall and leaves to put them away.

"What gives?" Ally questions her friend immediately.

"Sleuthing 101," Sam explains. "It's much easier to do it without someone looking over your shoulder. I just effectively got rid of our two biggest problems."

Grinning with appreciation, Ally gestures towards the two little girls still playing on the floor. "What about them?"

"These guys," Sam says lovingly, rolling the coveted ball across the floor towards them. "Can't talk in complete sentences."

Laughing now, Ally shakes her head. "That won't matter, because we aren't going to do anything that we aren't supposed to!"

"I never said we were," Sam agrees. "But if there *is* something mysterious here for us to find, this is the best way to do it. And we're going to start with learning the history behind that lighthouse."

4

SAND ON YOUR FEET & WIND IN YOUR HAIR

After having a late lunch of sandwiches and chips, Sam and Ally are cut loose to do what they want until suppertime. Although they already spent nearly an hour on the beach with the twins, they weren't able to go far, so it's promptly decided that exploring the beach is their first mission.

They quickly change into their swimsuits, then tiptoe past the room where the little girls are taking a nap and stop at the kitchen for a drink. Finding a water bottle, Sam fills it at the dispenser built into the fridge.

"Is it okay if we walk into town later?" Sam asks her mom, who is sitting in the adjoining family room, with her dad. They're going over a map of the area, and he's explaining where the marina is.

After a brief pause, Kathy looks at Ethan. "I don't see why not. Are you okay with that?" she asks her husband.

"It's probably no more than a ten or fifteen minute walk, on a residential street," he ponders. "Sure, so long as you don't go any farther than Main Street," he adds, turning his attention to Sam and Ally. "Everything you might want is located there. But beyond that is the main freeway, and there aren't sidewalks."

"We just want to check out the shops," Ally assures them. Taking her phone out, she holds it up for emphasis. "And maybe find some Wi-Fi?"

Laughing, Kathy smiles at her warmly. Ally is like a daughter to her, and she understands her perfectly. "I'm sure you can put those detective skills to good use and find it, if it's there."

Ally's grin falters at the suggestion that she *might* have to go yet another week this summer being disconnected from the rest of the world.

"Come on!" Sam urges, pulling at her arm. "We've got four hours until dinner. Let's go!"

Propelled by her friend's enthusiastic grip, Ally stumbles after Sam out the large glass sliding door off the dining area. Already familiar with the decking, the girls scamper down the two flights of weather-beaten steps and jump into the soft, warm sand.

Ally heads for the water, where they can see John and Hunter splashing around, but Sam veers off to the right.

"Where are you going?" Ally calls, while holding a hand up to her eyes to shield them from the bright afternoon sun.

"We can go in the water anytime! Let's see how close we can get to the lighthouse." Sam is walking backwards as she talks, and nearly trips over some driftwood. Laughing, she catches herself and then looks pleadingly at Ally. "Please?"

"Oh, okay," Ally agrees. "But there's no way we can walk all the way out there! It's got to be at least five miles, and I don't think your parents would be happy about it."

"We won't go that far," Sam reassures her. "I just want to see what's down this way, and look for anything…interesting." She says the last bit with a knowing twinkle in her eye, and Ally can't help but give in.

Running awkwardly in the heavy sand, Ally reaches Sam and then passes her, grabbing her towel out of her hand as she goes by. Crying out in mock anger, Sam does her best to catch up as Ally heads for the wet, compact sand.

The boys spot them and call out, but their voices are carried away by the wind. Ignoring them, they continue running the other way, towards the distant lighthouse. Although both Sam and Ally are athletic, the sand and stiff breeze take a toll quickly, and they don't get that far before slowing, and then finally walking.

"Here," Ally gasps, giving the towel back and freeing herself of the extra weight. Hands on hips, she breathes deeply while studying the stunning shoreline.

While the interior of the peninsula is all rainforest, here on the outer edges it changes back to your normal woods. Tall cedar trees mark the clear transition from beach to forest, bent over from years of offshore winds. The foliage becomes thick just a short distance in, making it hard to see what lies beyond.

"Look at how tall it is!" Sam exclaims, interrupting Ally's thoughts.

Turning, Ally sees that Sam is focused on the lighthouse. She's right, too. It's still a very long ways away, but it has to be close to a hundred feet high, reaching far up into the cloudless sky.

"Can you imagine what it must have been like to build that?" Ally wonders.

"Maybe we can find a library when we go into town, or a historical book at one of the shops," Sam suggests, finally looking away. "There's got to be some information about it there. Maybe they have tours, or something!"

A bit relieved that her friend is thinking along the lines of a guided tour, rather than an unapproved exploration on their own, Ally waves at the greenery behind them. "Even if we can't get into the lighthouse, I'll bet there are hiking trails around here!"

Seeming to notice the woods for the first time, Sam's smile spreads even wider. Throwing her arm around Ally's shoulders, she steers her towards them. "That's why I like you so much, Ally," she says sincerely. "You always know what will make me happy!"

Trudging awkwardly through the drifts of warm, heavy sand, they eventually reach the tree line. "We're going to need our shoes," Sam states, looking down at their bare feet.

Swinging the stuffed beach bag off her back, Ally pulls out their flip-flops and they quickly put them on before stepping onto the forest floor. Sam marvels at how quickly the scenery changes. Even the air is several degrees cooler in the shade of the huge trees.

"There's a sign up there!" Ally exclaims, picking up her pace. The two of them scamper through the foliage until they come to an obvious trailhead. It's clearly marked by an ancient looking, wooden sign.

"Caution." Sam reads the sign aloud. "Trail is not maintained. Use at your own risk." Chewing on her bottom lip, she looks at Ally with eyebrows raised.

"We shouldn't," Ally states, answering the unspoken question. "At least, not wearing bathing suits and sandals!"

"Don't you mean not before you ask Mom and Dad to make sure it's okay?"

Spinning around at the unexpected voice behind them, Sam and Ally are surprised to see Hunter and John standing there. Hunter's arms are crossed over his chest, and he's looking at them rather smugly.

"Mind your own business, Hunter!" Sam retorts, hands on hips.

"Whoa!" John says, hands held out in between the two of them. "He just means that it doesn't look that safe, Sam. It might not be a good idea to go traipsing in there without knowing where the trail goes."

"Come on, Sam." Pulling at Sam's elbow, Ally leads her best friend back towards the water and away from their brothers. "He's just trying to start an argument with you."

Giving the boys with a dirty look, Sam allows herself to be steered clear of them. As soon as she turns back to Ally, a smile replaces her scowl and they both laugh. Sparring with their brothers is a natural thing. It happens on a daily basis and certainly isn't enough to sour their moods.

"We might as well swim for a bit before heading into town," Sam suggests, kicking her shoes back off.

The girls leave a trail of clothes and towels behind them as they race to the water and plunge into the churning waves.

Having grown up on the coast, both girls are well aware of the dangers associated with ocean swimming. Although they are in a somewhat protected cove, there's still a risk of undertows and riptides, which are rivers of water under the surface that can quickly pull you out to sea. Watching the wave patterns with a practiced eye, Sam is careful to stay in waist deep water. They won't go out any farther until they're familiar with the area. For now, they'll just do some body-surfing, close to shore.

"I'll never get used to how cold it is!" Ally gasps, wrapping her arms around herself and shivering as the waves lap at her thighs. The water of the Pacific Ocean on the Washington coast never gets much above the mid-fifties. So even on a hot, late July day, it'll suck the heat out of you quickly. Unless you have a wetsuit, you're limited to spending a brief time near the shore, before having to warm up again.

"Wimping out already?" John shouts, as he runs past them with a boogie board. With a hoot, he flies through the air, splashing down into an incoming wave, and riding it to shore. Hunter is close behind him, and then the two jump back up to race into the next big swell.

"Who said anything about wimping out?" Sam calls, racing after them. After some begging, the boys let them use the boards, and the four of them spend the next hour soaking up the sun and saltwater.

Eventually, Sam and Ally drag their half-frozen bodies back up the beach and collapse in the baking sand. As the sensation slowly comes back to her fingers and toes, Sam turns over onto her stomach to seek out the source of a new sound. Finally spotting some movement in the shade of the house next to theirs, she nudges Ally.

"Huh?" Ally moans, her arms and legs splayed out.

"Check out our neighbors," Sam whispers, poking her in the ribs again.

Curious now, Ally shades her eyes against the sun and then rolls onto her stomach, too, to get a better look. Sure enough, in front of the only other house near them, a little girl that looks to be about six sits playing with a shovel and bucket. It's the cheap kind you can get for a couple of bucks, and the shovel has already broken so that sat she's forced to hold it down close to the scoop. The sound Sam had heard was the scraping of the sand, and then the soft thud of it landing in the bottom of the plastic container.

The little girl's long, blonde hair is loose and blowing wildly in the breeze so that she pauses frequently to pull it out of her eyes. Perhaps the lighting under the shade of the trees makes her appear paler than she is. Her face seems to glow in the shadows. Sensing that she is being watched, the girl looks up at them, and Ally is certain that she sees dark bags under her piercing blue eyes.

Pushing up to her knees, Sam waves a warm hello and smiles at her. She might be several years older than the twins, but they could still have a lot of fun playing together. When the girl doesn't wave back, Sam hesitates…but deciding to introduce herself, she stands and starts making her way over, Ally right behind her.

"Hi there!" Stopping at what they think is an acceptable distance, Sam and Ally stand just beyond the reach of the shade so that the sun still warms their backs. Sam doesn't see an adult anywhere, and she doesn't want to frighten the poor thing. Sam notes the hollow look on her young face and wonders what could possibly cause such a haunting expression on someone that age.

"My name is Sam, and this is Ally," she offers, pointing to herself first, and then Ally. "We're staying at the place next to you. What's *your* name?"

Looking back and forth between the two older girls, she drops the shovel, the large hole she was working on seemingly forgotten. Standing cautiously, she then looks first towards the smaller beach house behind her and then at the girls, eyes wide. *Is that fear?* Sam wonders.

"Are…are you okay?" Ally asks, apparently sensing the same thing as Sam. "Where's your mom?"

"I'm not supposed to talk to you!"

The whispered response is spoken with such terror, that Sam and Ally both take an involuntary step backwards, looking at each other with concern.

"Why can't you…" Before Sam can finish her question, a door on the back of the house bangs open, setting the little girl into motion. Spinning on her heel, she races up the steps leading to a small porch, her bare feet banging out a beat as she goes.

"Erica! What are you doing out here by yourself?" The man doesn't say it with menace, but concern, and he kneels down to embrace the girl approaching him. Erica dashes off to the side, avoiding his grasp. Instead, she runs behind him and grabs onto the leg of a breathtakingly beautiful woman leaning in the open door. Although wearing simple blue jeans and a non-descript, black top, she somehow appears regal. Full, slightly parted lips grace a flawless face, without a trace of make-up.

Reaching down, she absently rests a hand on Erica's blonde hair while holding Sam's gaze. Unsure of what to do, Sam raises her hand halfheartedly in another vain attempt at introductions. The dark-haired woman squints her eyes in reply, giving her head a slight shake before ushering Erica inside, the screen door slapping in their wake.

5

ODD NEIGHBORS

"Hello there, girls! My name is Kevin Moore."

Refocusing on the man now walking towards them, Sam tries to shake off the odd feeling the encounter has given her. He seems pleasant enough, and looks a bit embarrassed.

"I'm Sam, and this is Ally," Sam replies, accepting his now offered hand. "We're staying next door for the week," she adds quickly, feeling a bit awkward. He has a limp handshake, leaving her with an impression of insincerity.

"I feel like I have to apologize for my daughter, Erica," he adds, stepping out from the edge of the shade to join them in the sunshine. Slowly, he looks back and forth between them, as if making a point of addressing them both like adults. "She has…some behavioral issues. It's very difficult for her to communicate normally, and she needs constant supervision. I'm afraid my wife has taken to keeping them both somewhat isolated because of it. We've had a few episodes where Erica has wandered off and we even had to call the police to help find her. I thought a nice trip out here to the beach for a vacation might be relaxing, but it's been a bit of a trial. Erica isn't comfortable being away from home," he adds for extra emphasis, looking down with a gesture of defeat.

"Oh, that's okay!" Ally offers, reaching out to touch his arm encouragingly. "Don't worry about it. Sam here has two younger sisters Erica can play with, and I babysit all the time. We're used to kids behaving differently, so it doesn't bother us. I'm really sorry though that you're having such a hard time with her."

While Ally is quick to accept his explanation, Sam hesitates. There's something about the man that just doesn't sit right with her.

Crossing her arms over her chest, she gazes back at him when he looks up. Briefly, she sees an expression of annoyance flicker across his handsome features before breaking out in a warm smile.

"Thank you, Ally. It's nice that you understand. It's sometimes hard to fit in with a...troublesome child."

Turning to Sam, Kevin's smile falters slightly. "I wish that Erica could play with your sisters, Sam, but it would be too difficult. I hate to request this, but I think it best if everyone were to stay away for now, so that we don't upset her any more than she already is."

"Sure," Sam says. "Whatever you think is best, Mr. Moore. But my mom used to be a schoolteacher and she had several students with special needs. Maybe she could talk with your wife about it. She might be able to help."

Watching the man carefully, Sam notes his reaction as the fine lines on his face crinkle when his eyes narrow. A bit more of the friendly façade falls away, and his stance becomes rigid.

"My wife doesn't like company," he says flatly. "I hope you enjoy your stay, girls." With that, he turns abruptly without another word and walks back to the little house with long, purposeful strides.

"Well, that was weird," Sam eventually murmurs in his wake. She and Ally stand staring at each other for a moment, until a particularly big gust of wind swirls sand up and into their eyes, breaking the spell.

Turning their backs to the little dust devil swirling across the beach, they wipe at their faces and run to where their towels are spread out. The boys are still splashing in the water, having missed out on the encounter entirely.

"What do you think *that* was all about?" Ally asks, sitting down next to Sam. Digging her toes into the sand, she lets the sun erase the goosebumps from her arms.

"I dunno," Sam shrugs. Looking over her shoulder, she peers into the shadows surrounding the vacation home. "Mom always talked about how impressed she was with the parents of her special needs kids. Most of them were extra outgoing and involved in the classroom. I guess everyone is different though. If Erica really is that troubled, they might not have a choice. But…"

Raising her eyebrows, Ally looks more closely at her friend. "But what, Sam?"

"I don't trust him."

"Time to get wet!" Freezing cold water sprays over the girls at the same time that the boys call out to them. Screaming, they do their best to shield themselves with the towels, but they still end up half-soaked.

"Hunter!" Ally yells, covered once again in goosebumps. "I was finally getting warm!"

"Exactly why you needed to cool off," Hunter laughs, giving one final shake of his boogie board in their direction.

"I think it's time to go to town," Sam says quietly to Ally, not wanting their brothers to follow them. Pretending to run to the beach house to get dry, they go straight through and out the front door, waving at Kathy and the twins on the way.

Pulling their shorts out of the beach bag, they quickly slip them on over their swimsuits as they walk up the quiet, residential street. "We have less than a month until school starts," Ally declares, kicking at a pinecone. "I wish we could stay here. I'm not so sure I want to be in seventh grade."

Sam struggles to focus on what her friend is saying. Her mind is still trying to wrap itself around the odd behavior of their new neighbor. Looking sideways at Ally, she sees that the other girl's mood has changed drastically, and it surprises her. Sam had always thought Ally *enjoyed* school, and was looking forward to middle school. At least, that's how she acted around their other friends.

"What are you worried about?" Sam finally asks, her longer legs easily matching the quick pace that Ally is setting.

"Well, you saw what happened with our brothers, when John got into high school. It all changes, Sam," she says a bit more desperately, stopping suddenly. "What if that happens to us?"

Skidding to a halt and turning back to face Ally, Sam grasps her firmly by the upper arms. The spattering of freckles across her nose seems to stand out in starker contrast under the shade of the trees. "Ally, why are you worrying about this now?" Her brows furrowed, Sam tries to figure out what's really behind her friend's anxiety.

"It's all different, Sam." Breaking free of Sam's grasp, Ally starts walking again, but more slowly. "We know everyone at school, and we've been friends with most of them since kindergarten. But now…there's going to be a ton more kids at the middle school, and we won't know over half of them! We might not have *any* classes together, and what if we have a different lunch? You know they have two lunches, right?"

The elementary school for their small, seaside town consists of barely two-hundred kids, total. They have to be bussed to a central middle school in the next town over, where all of the incoming seventh graders arrive from neighboring districts. While it's a much different, larger setting, Sam still hadn't suspected that her popular, outgoing friend was worried about it.

"The class list should be up when we get back next week," Sam says, trying to think of something positive to add. When nothing good comes to mind, she decides to just be honest.

"Ally…I thought you loved school. I don't understand why you're so worried about it. You know that everyone is going to love you and you'll just have twice as many friends as before."

"I'm not worried about making new friends!" Ally says forcefully, pushing at a low-hanging branch. "I don't want to lose the ones I already have," she adds, looking down at her feet so that Sam barely hears her.

Now it's Sam's turn to stop. When Ally realizes she's no longer beside her, she turns back and is surprised to find Sam standing in the middle of the road, hands placed firmly on her hips.

"Ally, we're making a pact right now!" she announces. Now that she knows what her friend's fears are, it's easy to solve. At least, to *Sam* it seems obvious enough. "We're going to promise each other, that no matter what, we'll *always* be friends." Sticking her hand out for emphasis, she raises her eyebrows at Ally in expectation.

Unable to maintain her negative attitude in light of Sam's positive outlook, Ally grins and steps up to take her hand. "Best friends forever, 'till the end of time!" she declares with conviction.

"Until the end of time!" Sam repeats, making an exaggerated shake of their hands. But she doesn't let go. Instead, she pulls Ally close to her and gives her a fierce hug. "Till the end of time, Ally," she whispers into the fuzzy, red hair that she loves so much.

6

THE SECRETS OF
WOOD COVE

Sam's dad was right. It takes the girls less than fifteen minutes to reach the center of town. Standing once again in front of the curious statue, they glance around at the various stores. Although it's midafternoon on a Monday, there's still a sizeable crowd. Tourists come and go from the nearest gift shop, and they decide to start there.

A little bell hanging over the entrance announces their arrival, but no one behind the counter takes notice. They're too busy loading various trinkets into paper bags, after ringing them up on an antiquated register.

There's so much random stuff to choose from that it's overwhelming. Sam is fascinated by some dried seahorses, while Ally looks through the shop's shelves of T-shirts. The small space is crammed tight with merchandise, so it's hard to move around. Finally, after more than half an hour, they find a rack in the far corner that's full of brochures and pamphlets with local info.

"I found one!" Ally cries triumphantly, after looking through everything twice. Holding the small booklet out to Sam, she reads the title. "Wood's Cove Lighthouse - the history behind its construction and demise."

"Sweet! But how much is it? I didn't even think to bring money!" Sam pats at the empty pockets of her shorts.

"It's just two dollars," Ally answers. "I've got a few bucks on me."

Back at the counter, Sam is eager to learn more about the local legend. "So what can you tell us about that monster thing?" she asks the checker, while pointing out the window towards the carving.

Shrugging, the teen girl snaps her gum and

drops the book into a small bag. "Just a tourist thing," she answers, obviously bored by the conversation. "I wouldn't worry about it."

Unsatisfied with the response, Sam tries to push the issue, but the girl turns to help a couple of kids in line behind them. Clearly dismissed, she picks up their bag and follows Ally back outside. Taking the booklet out, they sit together on a small, wooden bench and thumb through it.

"There's nothing in here about Wood's monster," Sam says with disappointment. "It just gives some dry history on when the lighthouse was built. Apparently, it was constructed shortly after Mr. Wood founded the town in 1845, as a way to help guide the fishing vessels back into the cove. But it doesn't say anything about its condition *now*."

"At least it gives some background on the town," Ally says encouragingly. Holding the book up in front of her nose so she can read the small print, she clears her throat. "Mr. Wood and his wife settled in Wood's Cove in 1840, and it quickly became one of the largest fishing communities on the Washington coast at the time. To this day, the town still relies on the fishing industry for the bulk of its economy, second only to tourism."

"You're never going to learn the *real* story of Wood's Cove in a book, young miss." The dry cackle that follows the hoarse declaration is unnerving, causing both Sam and Ally to spin around in search of the source.

Leaning against a corner of the building is an old weathered man who has to be at least eighty years old. His pale blue eyes sparkle with intelligence as he slowly raises an antique-looking pipe to his lips. It's smokeless, so Sam guesses he's simply puffing on it out of habit. Her uncle, who lives in Montana, smokes sweet smelling pipes sometimes. But mostly, he'll just sit with an unlit one hanging from his mouth.

The dry laugh trails off, and he looks back and forth between the two expectantly. "Well?" he demands, sounding disappointed. "Aren't you going to ask me what I mean?"

Sam takes in his dirty, hole-ridden jeans and baggy white t-shirt. He stands stooped over so that he's barely taller than Ally. While his one hand holds the pipe, the other one tugs absently at his long, greasy grey beard. Wild hair frames his line-creased face and matches it in color, completing the old sea captain look. He just needs a sailor hat or bird on his shoulder…or something.

"So, what do you mean?" Sam asks good-naturedly while suppressing a laugh, having decided that he's most likely harmless.

Scrunching up his face in an exaggerated scowl, the old man seems to consider whether Sam is making fun of him. When Ally also smiles encouragingly at him though, he finally removes the pipe and breaks out in a wide, toothless grin.

"Old man Wood *did* create this town," the man croaks, waving the pipe around to encompass the surrounding buildings. "He was the best fisherman in these parts, and always brought his men home safely. That was largely due to Dead Man's Point Lighthouse," he continues, nodding to the distant structure barely visible through the trees.

"Dead Man's Point?" Sam interrupts, suddenly more interested in the story.

"Plenty of lives were lost to the rocks before the lighthouse was built," the old man explains, his voice even gruffer. "Not all of the captains were as good as Wood was. Even so, his time finally came, too." Pausing for dramatic effect, the storyteller slowly looks to Sam, and then Ally. "One particularly foggy night, the keeper failed to light the candle. Wood's ship bashed against the rocks and went down, but the captain was credited with getting her close enough to shore that all hands survived…except for him."

Looking morosely at his dirty feet, clad in slippers that appear as old as he is, he pauses again. Sam wonders how many times the man has told this sea tale to tourists, and suspects he'll want some form of compensation for it when he's done. Meeting Ally's gaze over the top of his bowed head, they share a knowing look. Ally winks slowly and jingles the change in her pocket, putting Sam's concern at ease.

"His body was never recovered!"

Startled by the sudden exclamation, Sam and Ally jump before giggling at themselves. Sam decides that she rather likes the storytelling abilities of their new acquaintance, and leans in to listen closely to rest of the folktale.

"Now, the captain had long told his story

of the cove monster," he continues, not disappointing them. "He claimed to see it often sliding just below the surface, keeping pace with the ship as it approached the entrance to the cove. While no one else saw it, they *did* hear an eerie sound on nights when there was an extra thick fog. Wood said it was his sea creature speaking to them, reminding them of his existence, and vowing to protect the cove. This is why it's believed by most that the sea creature took the captain to the depths below when he slipped into the water that night. Finally together, they continue to protect the cove and all the ships that come and go."

Mistakenly taking his silence as a sign that this is the end of the story, Sam starts to ask a question, but he quickly stops her with a raised hand.

"Every night after his disappearance until her death, the captain's wife walked the dark trail to the lighthouse, bringing a candle with her to light the way. She would climb the stairs and ensure that the lighthouse shone bright, convinced her husband would still find his way back to her. To this day," he continues, looking ever so seriously at both of the girls, "on foggy nights, you can hear the wail of the creature and see the dim light of the candle still shining at the top of the lighthouse, beckoning him home."

Delighted with the story, Sam and Ally clap when he finishes, and Ally gladly gives him all of her change. With a barely concealed moan at the small amount, he nonetheless drops it into his jeans pocket and starts to turn away.

"Wait!" Sam calls, stopping him. "How can we see inside the lighthouse?" she asks hopefully.

"That's not possible," he answers abruptly, shaking his head for emphasis. "It's over a hundred and fifty years old, and hasn't been used for nearly fifty of those. It was wired for electricity in the early nineteen hundreds, but it became too expensive to maintain. With the fancy equipment the new fishing boats had, it just wasn't needed anymore. When the trails were washed out from landslides and it became inaccessible other than by boat, the town committee decided they couldn't afford to keep it going. It's been sitting there falling apart ever since."

"Are you sure there's no other way?" Sam presses.

Ally gives her a warning look, afraid that her friend is already planning something dangerous.

"You'd do best to stay away from there," the old storyteller cautions, but with a new tone. No longer weaving a tale, he's standing a bit straighter and his words have a sharper edge. "There's nothing there for you to see. Nothing good has ever come from that place. Its walls echo with sorrow."

Surprised by his conviction, Sam watches as he walks away, mumbling something under his breath. Looking guiltily at Ally, she shrugs. "I just wanted to make sure, is all," she explains sheepishly. They begin to walk back the way they came, both of them silent as they think about the somber story.

Without warning, Ally throws her arm up in front of Sam to stop her. Looking sharply at her friend, Sam finds Ally has a finger to her lips to silence her retort, and mouths the word 'listen.' Taking a moment, Sam hears what seems to be a very heated conversation going on nearby.

Stepping a bit closer to the nearest building, they slowly edge towards the corner so they can look down the alleyway. Standing about twenty feet away is a group of three men, one of them waving his arms in anger as he speaks with a heavy accent.

"I don't care *how* much I'm paid, man. I didn't sign up for this!"

The man is dressed like any other tourist, but he's very large and has a dangerous look about him. Sam's eager to retreat, when she focuses on the guy he's talking to…and gasps. It's Mr. Moore!

Just as their neighbor starts to turn his head in their direction, Ally pulls Sam back, out of sight. Now worried the men sense someone listening, the girls run quickly in the opposite direction and duck into the nearest store.

Doing their best to walk calmly to the farthest corner, they find a big rack of stuffed animals to hide behind. Peeking between plush whales and starfish, the girls watch as Mr. Moore steps through the doorway and slowly looks around. Holding their breath for what feels like an eternity, he finally scowls before disappearing back outside.

7

BROTHERS!

Dinner is almost ready by the time Sam and Ally get back to the house. They hurry to help set the table while the boys assist with putting the final touches on the sandwiches.

A Philly Steak/French Dip combo is a favorite dish in the Wolf household, and Ally is always sure to be invited over when they have it. But it's been a while since John has eaten with them, and he makes it clear that he's missed it. Sam notes how he and Hunter have fallen right back into their familiar routine with each other, their constant banter light and easygoing.

Helping the twins into their highchairs,

Sam cuts up some grapes to put alongside their French fries. Grapes are one of the few fruits they'll eat, so they always try to have them handy. It's not unusual for a good portion of their meals to end up on the floor and getting them to eat is always a challenge.

"Find anything interesting in town?" Kathy asks, pouring water into the glasses they set out. "Any Wi-Fi?" she directs to Ally.

Groaning, Ally pats at the phone still in her pocket. With their unexpected encounters, she had completely forgotten to even check!

"I forgot," she admits dismally, looking at Sam with a little guilt. They weren't sure whether to share the encounter with Mr. Moore. It was dangerously close to snooping.

"So what happened?" John presses. "No way Ally wouldn't be jumping all over her phone unless something more interesting came up."

Ethan Wolf raises his eyebrows questioningly at the girls as everyone takes a seat at the big table. He knows his daughter well enough to interpret the furtive glances at her best friend. "So?" he finally asks when no one volunteers an answer.

While she might have been able to make excuses for not offering to tell her parents about Kevin Moore, now she doesn't have a choice. Sam might be curious and maybe a bit too bold when it comes to taking risks to help people, but one thing she won't do is lie.

"Well…" she starts, looking to Ally for input. When her friend returns a blank stare instead, Sam sighs in resignation. "We sort of….kind of…well, *almost* had a run-in with our neighbor, Mr. Moore."

"Who?" her mom asks. Her sandwich is paused halfway to her mouth, bits of roast beef, sautéed onions, and cheese oozing out the sides.

Realizing that her parents don't even know about the odd Kevin Moore and his family next door, Sam quickly explains the weird introductions from earlier in the day. She then recites the old fishing tale in detail, including a fairly decent imitation of the old man's voice that has the boys laughing. By the time she describes the scene in the alley though, and their hiding out in the gift shop, her parents aren't amused anymore.

"I'm disappointed that we're having this

conversation," Ethan admonishes. "Especially this soon into our trip."

"But Dad, we didn't *do* anything," Sam pleads.

"It's what you didn't do...like walk away. From now on, if you find yourself having to *hide* from view in order to listen or see something, just don't do it. Okay? Is that so hard?" Tapping his fingers on the table in beat to his words, it's obvious that her father is frustrated with them.

Hanging their heads, both of the girls nod in understanding and continue eating in silence.

It's not long before the quiet is interrupted by squeals of joy from Tabitha and Addison, who seem to be having a contest to see who can throw her grapes the farthest. Glad to have the distraction, Sam busies herself retrieving the food.

The commotion breaks up the awkward silence and the boys start telling them all about their day in the water, the new friends they made, and about a sand castle festival that's happening on the beach Friday.

Her scolding nearly forgotten in light of this exciting development, Sam sits back down in her chair and leans forward eagerly. "A *sand castle* festival?" she asks. "Do you mean the kind where they have contests and stuff?"

"Yup." Hunter answers before John can speak up. "We met these kids staying down the beach a ways, and they told us all about it. Happens every year. Sand castle building contest, food, music, swimming contests, paragliding and everything! I guess your old sea captain forgot to tell you, huh?" he adds mockingly, wiggling his eyebrows at his sister.

Doing her best to ignore the bait, Sam turns back to her mom. "That sounds like a lot of fun! We can go, can't we?"

Relieved that her daughter appears more interested in the festival than the local legend and mysterious neighbor, Kathy is more than happy to say yes. "It sounds like something the whole family can enjoy together. Good timing," she adds, turning to Ethan.

As they all start talking about it at once, Sam is reminded of the trail they discovered earlier in the day. With everything happening since, she had almost forgotten!

"Dad, would it be okay if Ally and I hike a

trail we found near the beach?" she asks when there is a break in the conversation. "It's marked with a sign and everything. We wouldn't go far."

"Do you mean the one with the sign that says not to use it because it's dangerous?" Hunter asks, a self-satisfied grin on his face.

At the look of disappointment her father turns on her, Sam can't help herself, and lashes back.

"It says no such thing, Hunter!" she fumes, eyes flashing. "It just cautions that the trail isn't maintained, is all. *Not* that it's dangerous. Stop trying to make it seem like I'm being sneaky!"

"All right. kids," Kathy warns, "that's enough. Hunter," she continues, turning to him and waving a fork in his direction for emphasis. "I know exactly what you're doing, and it isn't going to work. Stop trying to cause trouble."

His grin widening, Hunter goes back to finishing his second sandwich, satisfied that his input had the desired effect.

"Now Sam, you know how I feel about you going on random trails by yourself. Whether it says caution or danger doesn't really matter," her dad quickly adds, when she starts to argue.

"You and Ally are twelve years old, and while you have proven yourselves capable, I still don't agree with you running off to wherever you feel like. If you want to go on a hike, that's fine. But you'll either wait until I'm done with my work and available, on Sunday before we leave. Or you can take the boys with you."

With that declaration, Hunter and John exchange a knowing smile and it's all Sam can do to not blurt out what she thinks. Biting her tongue, she reaches under the table and nudges Ally's leg, cautioning her. While Sam is the more vocal of the two, she wouldn't put it past Ally to say something to her brother. They have to be careful. They've been in trouble too many times before and it wouldn't take much to get them grounded.

"Okay, Dad," Sam finally says evenly, surprising everyone. With satisfaction, she watches the smiles fall from both Hunter and John's faces, and reaches casually for more french fries. "I understand. We won't go without you or the boys. Do we still get to go to the marina with you in the morning?"

During the drive to the cove, he invited them to visit where he'd be working for the week. Sam has always been fascinated with the different fishing boats, and she's been looking forward to exploring the new marina. When her dad nods in confirmation, obviously surprised by her lack of argument about the trail, she feels a twinge of excitement.

If there was a good spot to learn more about Old Captain Wood and his sea monster, it's where all the current fishermen hang out. Ally returns the nudge under the table, and Sam figures she's thinking the same thing. A small prickle crawls up the base of her spine. She knows without a doubt that their trip is about to get more interesting!

8

EXPLORING THE
MARINA

Early the next morning, Sam sits in the front seat of the van, next to her dad. She yawns loudly. Her optimism about the day ahead isn't quite as positive as it was last night, but that's only because the sun has just started to break above the waterline. She wishes now that she and Ally had gone to bed the *first* time her dad hollered at them to be quiet last night. But it was nearly impossible to fall asleep with the waves crashing outside, and the silhouette of the lighthouse visible in the moonlight, through the thin curtains.

When the warm sunshine reaches them on the narrow road that winds along the shore, Sam turns her face into it and finally smiles. It'll be worth it. The boys opted to stay behind and get the beach to themselves, although they'll have to watch the twins for a while. With her dad occupied with his work, and no one else to bother them, she and Ally should be able to do some sleuthing. Is there really a sea creature? Is there a way to get to the lighthouse? And who were those scary-looking guys that Mr. Moore was arguing with? Sam has been around marinas enough to know that in a small fishing town, *that's* where you go for answers, *not* the local tourist trap.

In less than twenty minutes, they pull into a massive parking area, and Sam is *not* disappointed. It's a huge harbor, with dozens of large commercial fishing vessels mixed among smaller, private boats. There's at least one restaurant, a tackle shop, a rental store and numerous smaller booths housing various wares.

Turning in her seat to point out the shops to Ally, Sam sees the wide-eyed expression on her friend's face. Although they live by the ocean and there's a marina there at home, she's never seen anything quite like this before.

"I didn't think it'd be this *big*," Ally says in awe, looking around as they get out of the van. "Where do all these people come from?" she asks, as they dodge out of the way of a group walking by at a brisk pace.

Ally is right; the population here is likely higher than in town. "A lot of them live on their boats," Sam explains, looking to her father for confirmation.

"That's right, Sam," he agrees, directing them towards what must be the main office. "I imagine a fair amount of them live here year-round. You have to keep in mind that most of the town's population also works here in one aspect or another. Add to that the commercial vessels that come and go on a regular basis, and you get quite the gathering. One of the reasons my boss chose Wood's Cove for the work on his boat is because of the particular craftsmanship that's needed. It's very hard to find nowadays, almost a lost art. Some of the woodworkers here have been doing it their whole lives. You just can't hire the same kind of help anywhere."

Following closely behind her dad, Sam holds onto Ally's hand so they aren't separated in the throng of people. It's barely seven in the morning, but the place is awash with activity and noise. Huge cranes lift crates of fish from ships to waiting transport, the men barking out orders from all directions. Workers tromp past them on the boardwalk, going about their tasks with a single-minded purpose. Vendors move at a slower pace, setting out their goods with a practiced ease and waving as the workers go by, recognizing them as potential customers.

Once inside the large, main building, the marina noise is replaced with a different variety of sounds altogether. Ringing phones, tapping keys and intense conversations fill the space, echoing so that it's even more disorienting than the scene outside.

It's not long before a tall, silver-haired man greets Ethan, shaking his hand enthusiastically. They're obviously at the right place. After a brief discussion, the man leads them all back out onto the main dock and towards one of the larger ships, moored at the end. When they reach the gangway leading to the deck several feet above them, Ethan turns to the girls and leans in so they're sure to hear him.

"I've got business to take care of now," he explains, motioning to the boat behind him. "It's going to be a lot of boring paperwork at first, checking over all of the documentation to make sure everything's on track and accounted for. But here," he continues, taking out his wallet. "There's enough to explore to keep you busy for hours, Sam. Find some souvenirs for everyone," he continues, handing her some money. "Let's meet in front of that big restaurant at noon. After we eat, I'll be able to give you guys the full tour of this beast here, once I'm familiar with it. Deal?"

Smiling broadly, Sam takes the cash and looks around at all of their options, unsure where she wants to start. The atmosphere reminds her of a carnival. Mixed with the salty, crisp sea breeze, it's energizing. "Sure, Dad!" she exclaims, bouncing on the balls of her feet. "Don't worry about us!"

Her dad's grin falters slightly as he suddenly questions if it's wise to leave the girls to their own devices. Sam can tell he's about to suggest a new plan, but the silver-haired man looks back to see what's keeping him and calls out impatiently. Shrugging, Ethan finally turns and hurries to catch up.

"Phew! That was close," Ally observes. "I thought he might make us sit in some remote corner of that boat for the rest of the morning."

Laughing, Sam tugs at her arm and then walks quickly back down the long dock. "Nah…we could have talked him out of it. I've been coming to places like this with him for years now. It's not like we can get lost or anything, and most of the people here are honest workers, not trouble makers."

Not completely convinced, Ally studies a scary looking group of men clustered around a breakfast vendor. They look as if they haven't shaved for weeks, and their clothes are ragged and filthy. One of them turns, as if sensing her stare, and smiles broadly at her, exposing several missing teeth. Blushing furiously, Ally stumbles back into Sam and nearly causes them both to fall over.

Sam laughs as she catches her friend and

whispers in her ear. "They're just fishermen, Ally," she explains. "They've been out on the boat working for weeks straight. See their waders and boots?" she points out, nodding at their specialized gear. "Some of them might look a bit shady, but they have certain codes they live by around here. We don't need to worry."

Deciding that the food smells good, they take the men's place after they walk away and order breakfast burritos. It takes some time, but Ally eventually relaxes when no one attempts to kill them. By mid-morning, she's having as much fun as Sam is.

Every booth has something unique to offer, and the girls are entranced by the assortment of boats anchored along the maze of interlocking docks. They could easily spend the whole day just looking at them, and still not see them all.

By eleven-thirty, they've made their way to the far end of the boardwalk, and end up finding the perfect gift for the twins. This particular saleslady has a variety of inexpensive trinkets geared for children. Holding up two slightly different bouncy balls, Sam turns them in the sunlight. Inside the clear plastic, starfish light up when the ball is tapped or bounced.

"Those are very unique!"

The deep voice makes Sam jump. She spins around to find their neighbor, Kevin Moore, standing there.

"Umm, yeah…" Sam stammers, unsure if he's aware that the two of them were spying on him the day before. "I thought that my little sisters would like them."

"Oh, absolutely!" he says pleasantly. "I think that I'll pick one up for Erica, too. She loves toys that have flashing lights or glow in the dark."

While Mr. Moore is going out of his way to be polite, Sam detects an edge just below the surface, making his friendliness feel forced. But he was that way when they first met him on the beach, too. Perhaps it's just the way he is all the time.

After paying the woman her two dollars, Mr. Moore tosses the ball up and then snatches it out of the air dramatically before turning back to the two girls. "Enjoy your afternoon, ladies," he says grandly, nodding to each of them before walking away.

Without a word, Sam buys the two toys and then hurriedly guides Ally around the backside of the booth. Groaning, she follows, but drags her feet, suspecting what her friend is up to.

"We *can't* follow him again!" Ally protests.

"We're not," Sam answers. "We're just walking back towards the restaurant where we're supposed to meet my dad. If we happen to see where Mr. Moore goes…" Lifting her hands in a 'so-what' gesture, she looks sideways at Ally.

"So the fact that we're walking *behind* the booths has nothing to do with trying not to be seen?" Ally counters with disdain.

"Wait!" Sam suddenly mutters, putting out a hand to stop Ally. "Look!"

Reluctantly, Ally looks to where Sam is pointing. Sure enough, Mr. Moore is talking with the same two men he met in the alley the day before. Although she can't help but think they're doing something wrong, she feels a twinge of excitement and moves in closer to Sam.

Hidden among dozens of other people, they watch silently as the group moves down one of the smaller docks and stops at a boat near the end. The two strangers board first, and then Kevin follows, looking around suspiciously before disappearing inside the craft.

"If he's really here on vacation, then what's he doing with those guys?" Ally whispers, forgetting to feel guilty.

"Well, he isn't buying fish," Sam declares, unafraid of being heard this far away. "That's not a fishing boat and those aren't fishermen. It's not a houseboat either, so I doubt they're local. In fact," she continues, walking several feet out onto the dock. "It looks like it's a custom build. Very expensive." Studying the forty or so foot vessel from afar, Sam squints in the early afternoon sun. "I wish we could get a peek inside."

Before Ally has a chance to object to *that* idea, the men re-emerge and walk back towards them. They're so engrossed in their conversation, that Mr. Moore doesn't even notice them when they pass within five feet of each other. Exchanging a look of relief, Sam and Ally naturally walk the other way…and towards the boat.

When they come alongside it, Sam looks

back just in time to see the men go inside the restaurant, the same one they'll be eating at soon. "I'm just going to see if that porthole is covered or not," she tells Ally, scooting in close to the impressive boat. It has a two-story upper deck, with gold-trimmed portholes spaced every few feet, so they're almost eye level with them on the dock.

Without waiting for a response from her friend, Sam leans out over the gap, bracing her hands to either side of the window, the water sparkling several feet below. Inside, she can just make out a table made of rich mahogany, with several laptops and papers strewn across it.

Pushing back, Sam moves to the next porthole, closest to the ramp leading down to the deck. Unlike the large fishing boat, this one sets below the dock. But as she leans forward, one of the bouncy balls crammed into the pocket of her sweatshirt breaks free and bounces away. Gasping, Sam spins to grab it but misses, watching in dismay as it rolls down the footbridge and into the boat.

"Oh no!" Ally cries, peering in the window next to Sam.

They watch helplessly as the lights flash inside the ball while it rolls across the floor and then comes to rest under the table.

"When Mr. Moore sees that, he's going to think we went inside!"

"I'll just go grab it. Stay here," Sam says hurriedly, already rushing towards the ramp.

Once inside, Sam's eyes quickly adjust to the dim lighting, and she crosses the small but lavishly decorated living area. Beautiful wood trim is everywhere, buffed to such a shine that it almost looks fake. Sam has seen boats like this before on tours, and knows how much they cost.

Not slowing down to admire the work, she squats at the table and reaches blindly for the ball that stopped flashing. Her eyes are level with the table, making it impossible not to notice the odd documents on top. *I'm not really snooping,* she tells herself, as her hand closes over the ball and she scoops it up. *Not if I just happen to notice something during a totally innocent act.*

The papers are covered with long strings of math equations and diagrams of odd, hexagonal structures. At the top of each sheet is a logo, a simple design she's seen before, but can't quite place. The letters W and M are written in fancy text above and below the image.

Before she can look more closely, she hears the unmistakable sound of heavy footfall behind her. A flood of fear begins in the pit of her stomach and quickly spreads. Turning, her worst fears are confirmed as she sees the two unknown men blocking the light of the entrance, Ally cowering before them.

"Which one of you wants to explain what it is you're doing on my boat?" the largest one growls threateningly.

9

A CHANCE ENCOUNTER

Her mouth suddenly dry, Sam tries to swallow but nearly chokes on her fear. Up close, the two middle-aged men are even more intimidating. Both are large, with a polished and dangerous look. Not like common street criminals, but smart, with a hard edge. The man who spoke is closest to Sam. He's wearing what appear to be brand new clothes, from a local shop. She notices his boots aren't even broken in.

"Well? Speak up!" he demands, his blue eyes flashing. He has a thick accent, which Sam can't quite place. German? Russian?

Her paralysis finally broken, Sam stumbles

away from the table and trips over something on the floor, nearly falling at the man's feet. Putting her hands out to catch herself, she grabs onto a bag that's now tangled in her feet. Sam vaguely registers that it's a backpack…the type kids use for school. It has a bright tie-dye design. Clipped to the outside of it is a cellphone, encased in a bejeweled holder with the name 'CARRIE' carefully printed on it with a marker.

Blushing furiously, Sam struggles to her feet and focuses her attention on the men blocking the exit. "I'm really sorry, s…sir," she stutters. "I was getting this ball." She holds out her hand, revealing the bouncy ball inside. "Honest. It fell out of my pocket and rolled in here," she rushes, near tears.

The words continue to pour out, running together until Sam isn't even sure they can understand what she's saying. "It went under the table, and I was going to get it and leave. I promise we weren't doing anything else. I'm really, really sorry," she says again, looking back and forth frantically between the two hardened faces.

Evidently unsure what to think, the man

who seems to be in charge looks over his shoulder at the other guy, who shrugs, but remains silent. When he turns back to Sam, she gives the ball a little squeeze, causing it to light up. Perhaps it can somehow help prove their innocence. A slight spasm tugs at the corner of his mouth and Sam prays that he's fighting against a grin.

"Get outta here!" he finally orders, stepping aside to allow them to pass. "If I ever catch you near my boat again, I'll turn you into the harbormaster and let *him* deal with you!"

"Yes sir," Sam mumbles, looking down at her feet. "I'm sorry," she repeats one more time, before grabbing a still-frozen Ally and dragging her up the gangplank. Almost running now, they make it onto the dock and head straight for the restaurant.

Finally daring to look back, there's no sign of the men *or* Mr. Moore. Thank goodness he hadn't returned to the boat with the other men, or things might have been a whole lot worse. If they had made a scene with the harbormaster, it could have jeopardized her dad's job there.

"What if they tell that Moore guy, and

then *he* tells your parents?" Ally whispers, voicing Sam's fear.

"Then we'll probably be on the first bus back home," Sam answers morosely. "What was I *thinking?*" she moans, finally stopping. They're in the spot her dad told them to wait, but there's no sign of him yet. "Why didn't I just leave the ball? Sometimes I wish I'd stop doing things without thinking first," she adds, crossing her arms over her chest and looking at Ally.

"*I'm* the one who said we'd get in trouble if they found the ball," Ally adds, trying to point out that it's not all Sam's fault. "Besides, It's not like we really did anything wrong. They probably won't even tell Mr. Moore. Why would they?"

Sam tries to think about the situation rationally. Ally's right, the men have no idea that the girls are staying in the beach house next to Mr. Moore. They've never even seen them before. They're just a couple of kids getting a lost ball. It might not be so bad, after all.

"Sam! Ally!"

Expecting the worst, Sam spins around, but finds her dad waving at them and smiling happily. Relaxing, she lets out a big breath she didn't realize she was holding. "Hey, Dad!" she says in return, hoping she sounds normal.

Ushering them inside the restaurant, Ethan leads them to a booth and announces that they can have whatever they want to eat. Sam figures things must be going well with work.

After ordering burgers, onion rings and milkshakes, Sam and Ally sit back and listen politely to Ethan's detailed descriptions of the project he's overseeing. It's normally the kind of stuff Sam likes discussing with her dad. But the nagging guilt she's battling is preventing her from enjoying it.

Several times during the conversation, she's tempted to interrupt and tell him about her poor decision to go onto the boat. But he's in such a good mood that she can't bring herself to do it. *I'll tell him later,* she promises herself. *On the way back to the beach house.*

After they finish eating, Sam's dad takes them on an hour-long tour of the fishing vessel. It's massive, and by the time they're through, Ally has a better understanding as to why Sam is so fascinated by it. There are nearly a dozen workers spread out, performing various tasks. It's Ethan's job to make sure they're all on track and able to have it completed in time for the coming season.

The two girls are turned loose with a few more hours to kill before her dad is done for the day. Sam's anxiety has finally settled enough that she's starting to relax, but as soon as they walk back out onto the dock, it comes back with a vengeance.

"Look!" Ally urges, elbowing Sam in the ribs and then pointing out towards the marina.

Sam follows the direction of Ally's arm, sure that the harbormaster must be barreling down on them. She doesn't even know what he looks like, but she imagines he's large, with a patch over his eye. To her surprise, she sees a very distinctive boat heading out to sea instead.

"They're leaving!" Sam exhales, all the stress of the past couple of hours going with it. "They must not have reported us."

"Well, they said they wouldn't unless they caught us snooping again," Ally reminds her, always the rational one. "I'm sure it was no big deal to them."

Her mood vastly improved, Sam smiles and starts to skip back towards the vendor area.

"Come on!" she calls, waving for Ally to follow. "Let's go see if we can find out more about the Wood's Sea Creature or the lighthouse!"

They spend the remainder of their time browsing the rest of the businesses and talking with some of the locals. Well, those who were *willing* to talk to them. Most either laugh or wave them away at the mention of the old legend, but one lady in particular is helpful. She runs a small booth filled with small, hand-carved wooden figurines, and is likely even older than the man from town. Everything from seagulls to whales lines the shelves, but the item that catches Sam's attention is identical to the large statue in the town square.

On the ride back to the beach house, Sam rolls the replica of the sea creature around in the palm of her hand. The woman's tale had been almost identical to the old man's, with one important addition. After selling Sam the trinket for just a few dollars, she'd given them a dire warning: "Stay away from the beach at night, or you might end up in the beast's belly, too," she cackled, her voice harsh. "And the lighthouse!" The woman had directed the last statement pointedly at Sam, who'd been hounding her with questions about the structure. "It's cursed! There's a reason the town council voted unanimously not to repair the trails. You'd be smart to mind the signs and stay away."

Sam looks out the window at the passing scenery, now starting to look familiar. The woman's voice echoes through her thoughts. Could there really be something to the story of the haunting? *Does* Mrs. Wood's ghost return to the lookout, trying to lead her husband home?

Fighting rising goosebumps, Sam looks sideways at her dad and briefly considers telling him about their encounter on the boat. Now that the threat of being found out has passed, it doesn't seem as important. In fact, it all feels somewhat silly, and she wonders why she was even so upset about it. If she were to tell him now, he would feel obligated to track the boat owners down and apologize himself. It would make him look bad, and possibly spoil his whole week.

No, Sam decides. *I'm not going to let something that I did ruin this job for my dad. He doesn't need to know.*

Feeling better about things, Sam's step is a bit lighter when they get back. Everyone had a good day, and they all exchange stories over dinner that evening.

Sam and Ally go to bed early, having had just a few hours of sleep the night before. Setting the odd-looking sea creature on the nightstand next to the bed, Sam falls asleep staring at it, wondering if something like it could actually exist.

***

Waking with a start, Sam sits up abruptly and looks around the dark room, confused. It takes a moment to shake the weird images of sea monsters from her head and remember where she is.

"It was just a dream," she whispers to herself, looking over at the figurine to assure herself that it wasn't real. Getting up from the soft bed, she walks quietly over to the big, double glass doors that lead to the balcony. The room is stuffy, and she desperately needs some fresh air.

Pushing the doors open, Sam steps out into the blessedly cool, nighttime air. Leaning against the railing, she becomes fully awake, the dream already almost forgotten. Looking out at the beach, she can hardly see the water in the oily blackness. The moon lends little light as it's hidden behind a solid wall of thick fog rolling in off the crashing waves.

Beginning to shiver from the dramatic change in temperature, Sam turns to go back inside, but pauses when she hears an odd sound. Straining to hear it, she tilts her head and closes her eyes. There! Mixed in with the booming surf is a high-pitched wail unlike anything she's ever heard before. Eyes flying open, she turns to where she knows the lighthouse stands in the distance. To her astonishment, a dim light glows in the dark!

10

TRAIL OF CONFUSION

The sound still haunts Sam the next morning as she absently eats a big bowl of cereal. She'd dragged Ally out of bed the night before, but by the time they got out on the deck, both the wailing *and* the light were gone. Half convinced now that she'd still been dreaming, Sam's reluctant to tell anyone else about it. Her brothers would tease her for months!

It had taken a long time to fall back asleep with the weird mix of thoughts tumbling around in her head. Only Ally's threat of pouring water on her face finally got her up.

Already after nine, her father left for work

hours ago. The twins are outside with the boys, playing in the sand. Her mom has left a note on the table, explaining that she's gone into town.

Sam considers the events of the past two days. "I think we need to try and forget about our neighbors and all of this other weird stuff," she finally says, looking hopefully at Ally. "Let's just try to have fun today."

Surprised by the uncharacteristic announcement by her friend, Ally lowers her own spoon and stares back at her. The whole experience last night must have scared Sam more than she's willing to admit. Eager to help put her at ease, Ally nods in agreement. "I think that's a great idea, Sam," she says lightly. "It's a perfect day outside! We can spend it working on our tans."

By the time Sam's mom returns home, the boys have left to go swimming with their new friends, and Sam and Ally have taken over watching the twins. They're happy to unload the groceries and make lunch while Kathy gets the two-year-olds changed and ready to eat.

It's close to one in the afternoon when the girls finally get to spread their towels out and fulfill their goal for the day. Tabitha and Addison are down for their afternoon nap, so they don't even have to worry about them. And their older brothers won't be bothering them for a while.

"I saw a sign in town the other day for a theatre," Ally says lazily. "Do you think your parents would let us go to a movie later?"

"I don't see why not," Sam answers, propping herself up on her elbows. "Maybe Dad would let John take us all in the van? He's past his probation, isn't he?" In the state of Washington, the rules for teen drivers are strict. For the first six months, they aren't allowed to drive anyone that isn't a family member unless there's an adult present.

"Yeah, he's been able to drive his friends around for a couple of months now, but Mom and Dad have their own set of rules. Taking us to the movies would be fine, though."

"Do you think it'd be worth it?" Sam asks, biting at her lower lip. "Or would they torment us through the whole show?"

"Nah…John isn't like that anymore," Ally counters. "We'd sit far away from them, anyway. I think it'd be fun!" Agreeing to look into what movies were playing later that afternoon, they spend the next hour sweating under the blazing summer sun until they can't stand it anymore. Even with their existing tans and generous amounts of sunscreen, they're starting to burn.

Running for shade, they end up walking along the edge of the woods and soon find themselves at the mysterious trailhead. To Sam's surprise, she isn't that tempted to explore it. Intuition tells her that there's a very real danger involving that lighthouse. She's learned to listen to her instincts. Normally, she would at least suggest they walk parallel to the trail for a little ways, so that they could see what was around the first bend without really *going* on it. Her curiosity stirs a bit at that thought, but her brother abruptly interrupts it.

"Did you already forget what Dad told you, Sam?" Hunter announces loudly right next to her ear, causing her to jump. Laughing at her reaction, he takes a few steps onto the overgrown path and then turns back. "What's the matter? Feeling a bit guilty at being caught trying to break the rules?"

"We weren't even *on* the trail, Hunter!"

Ally shouts, stepping forward.

Both Hunter and John look at her in silence, startled by the venom in her voice.

"We don't even want to go to the lighthouse anymore...not after what happened last-"

Sam reaches for Ally, but fails to stop her in time from saying too much. She gives Ally a warning look, letting her friend know she doesn't want to talk about it.

"What happened?" John asks,

"Nothing," Sam replies, much too quickly.

"No...really," Hunter urges, without any hint of sarcasm. "What did you hear?"

Staring at her older brother, Sam notes the way he's shifting from foot-to-foot, looking over his shoulder into the woods nervously. Something's spooked him, too. "Wait," she says, as Hunter's last question sinks in. "What makes you think that we *heard* something?"

John and Hunter exchange a look, obviously trying to decide what to tell the girls. "Because we had a strange...experience the first night we were here," John finally says.

"How?" Ally presses, hands firmly planted

on her hips. "Your room is on the back of the house, *away* from the water."

Again, the boys hesitate. Running his hands through his blonde hair in frustration, John shrugs sheepishly. "The guys we met on Monday invited us to go body surfing by moonlight," he admits. "They're good guys," he's quick to add, when he sees shock register on the girls' faces as they realize that their brothers had snuck out. "They live here, and do it all the time, but we knew your parents probably wouldn't approve so rather than ask and be told no…we just, well…we just went."

"We aren't going to go again," Hunter tells them, cutting off the expected reprimands. "It's no big deal, we were just swimming. But…" He looks over his shoulder again, into the woods. "After about an hour, this thick fog started to build up, totally blocking the moonlight so we couldn't see very well. The other guys got all weird and said we had to go. On our way back, there was this bizarre wailing sound."

"At first, we thought someone might be in the water and need help," John says, picking up the story. "But when we stopped and tried to figure out where it was coming from, it was like it was all around us, in the fog. Freakiest thing I ever heard. We ran the rest of the way back!"

Sam is encouraged by the story, and shares her own experience from the night before.

"I didn't see any lights out there," Hunter says to Sam, gesturing in the direction of the lighthouse. "But I didn't really look, either."

After a moment of silence, Ally shakes her head. "I know that I'm the only one who hasn't heard it," she begins. "But don't you all think you're letting the whole sea legend thing get the best of you? It's got to be some sort of strange atmospheric thing involving the fog, and shape of the cove, and maybe the waves on the rocks or something."

Impressed with Ally's rational explanation, Sam is just glad that someone else *did* hear it, so she knows that she isn't going crazy. "Whatever it is," she says, stepping up to loop an arm through Ally's, "it's definitely interesting!"

Chuckling now at their fear, it's easy for the boys to imagine that it wasn't all that bad, while standing in the daylight. "So we were going to explore this trail now," John says, happy to change the subject. "You can come with us, if you want."

"Nah," Hunter mocks. "Look at 'em," he says to John. "They're too scared."

Almost relieved to have her brother behaving more like his normal self, Sam takes the bait. "We'll just see which one of us is *really* scared!" she retorts, pushing past him to lead the way. Ally has no choice but to follow, her arm still securely locked in Sam's.

Within minutes, they're transported to a different world, one filled with evergreens covered in hanging moss, and dense underbrush. Unlike the woods they were in at camp that had little groundcover other than dried pine needles, the rain forest has a spongy surface filled with ferns and moss. Fallen, rotting trees are hosts to huge mushrooms.

Any fears quickly forgotten, Sam and Ally race along the narrow path dappled in sunlight, where it manages to break through the canopy overhead.

After half an hour, the level trail begins to climb uphill. Before long, it becomes obstructed with deadfall and small rockslides. Still in their sandals, the girls struggle to get through.

"Maybe we should wait for the guys to catch up," Ally suggests. Standing with one foot up on a particularly large boulder in the middle of the trail, she looks back the way they came. Nearly falling off the top of a huge log she's climbing over, Sam is about to agree when she's interrupted by someone yelling for help!

"Please! If anyone can hear me....*help*!" It's the voice of a woman, and it isn't that far ahead of them. Spinning around towards the source, Sam doesn't wait for Ally, but starts running awkwardly up the slope.

"I'm coming!" Sam shouts, her feet slipping. She nearly falls as she reaches the crest.

"Carrie!" This time it's a little girl screaming the name in desperation. "Carrie!" she cries again, drawing closer.

Sam can hear footsteps coming towards her, and is shocked when the little girl from next door suddenly comes into view. Her blonde hair is matted to her face, stuck there by mud and tears.

"Erica?" Sam says in disbelief.

"Oh...I thought you were Carrie." The

small child says in dismay. Fresh tears course down her pale cheeks.

"Who's Carrie?" Sam asks, kneeling down in front of Erica and gently taking her by the shoulders.

"My sister," Erica whispers, looking back the way she had come. "We're trying to find her."

"Who?" Sam presses, as Ally joins them, looking bewildered by the scene. "Where's your mom? Is she the one calling for help?"

"Mommy!" Erica jerks away from Sam, as if remembering why she was running. "She fell, trying to find Carrie. Can you help her?"

Taking the girl by the hand, Sam leads her back up the trail. "Of course we will! Show us where she is, Erica."

It doesn't take long to reach the top of the slope, where it opens up to expose a huge bluff nearly bare of trees, overlooking the ocean far below. To the right is a vertical cliff of jagged rock protruding far above them.

Originally, the trail had followed a narrow span of dirt at the base of the rocks, cut into the hillside. To the left of it, a steep slope descends a couple of hundred feet down to the water. At one time, it allowed a fairly wide surface to walk across to the other side, where it disappears back into the trees. However, at some point, a massive rock and mudslide washed it out, leaving behind a dangerous course to navigate.

Shading her eyes against the sudden onslaught of sunlight, Sam tries to find the source of the cries for help, which have gotten fainter. Unbelievably, she sees Erica's mom about halfway across the destroyed trail. She must have been trying to get to the other side when she lost her footing, and nearly plunged to her death. The only thing that saved her is a rotten-looking branch of a tree that was knocked over and caught up in the slide. Her body is tangled up in it a few feet from the top, precariously balanced, and with no way to get back up.

Without even thinking about what she's doing, Sam orders Ally to keep Erica there, and then runs out onto the cliff.

11

A DARING RESCUE!

Stepping cautiously over the slippery rocks and debris, Sam quickly makes her way towards the woman. She does her best *not* to look down, but once she reaches the spot where Erica's mom slid off, she no longer has a choice. Lying flat on her stomach, Sam inches towards the edge and then peers down into her terrified face.

"Where's Erica?" she croaks, her voice hoarse from either yelling or fear.

"She's okay," Sam reassures her. "My friend Ally has her. I'm Sam...we kind of met the other day, but I don't know your name."

"Lisa," the woman says, somewhat

reluctantly. "I don't know how much longer the dead branch will hold me," she adds urgently, looking first at the limb under her, and then at the ocean and rocks far below. Staring back up at Sam desperately, a small whimper escapes her and a lone tear spills down her cheek. Even covered in dirt, with her long dark hair a frantic mess...she's one of the most beautiful women Sam has ever seen. Her large, emerald green eyes are bright and full of intelligence, demanding attention.

"I'm afraid to move," she tells Sam, which explains why she hasn't tried to pull herself back up. She's located just a couple of feet down, but if the branch were to snap under her weight, there's a good chance she would plummet to her death.

Reaching down as far as she can without slipping off the trail herself, Sam barely touches Lisa's outstretched hand. Grabbing it firmly, she tries to pull, but it's immediately obvious that Sam won't be able to lift her. She tries to get ahold of the black t-shirt Lisa's wearing, with her other hand, but it's short-sleeved and she just can't reach it. Her weight shifting under the strain, Sam starts to panic at the hopeless situation and her own danger.

Suddenly, a much larger hand covers hers in a strong grip, and Sam looks up in surprise at John, who's stretched out beside her. She was so focused that she hadn't heard him approach. Then, she's practically lifted off the ground when Hunter grabs her securely around the waist, preventing her from slipping any farther. Working together, the three of them manage to lift Lisa to safety while Ally and Erica watch anxiously.

Panting from the effort, Sam smiles at her brother and John, who are crouched on either side of her, then turns her attention to Lisa. The older woman is slowly getting to her feet. Having spotted her daughter, she's intent on reaching her. Without a word to her rescuers, she walks off on wobbly legs. Sam scrambles to follow to make sure she doesn't fall again.

Did she hit her head or something? Sam wonders, noting her odd, disjointed behavior.

As soon as they're back on solid ground, Ally releases Erica's hand, and the little girl runs to her mother. Kneeling down, Lisa gathers her up and starts murmuring to her that everything is okay.

"What happened?" Sam asks gently.

Looking at her again with those piercing green eyes, Lisa glances towards the lighthouse…visible from the bluff, but still a good distance away. Without a word, she stands and clearly forces all emotion from her features. Tugging once at Erica's hand, they begin to walk away.

"Wait!" Sam persists, remembering what the little girl had said. "What about Carrie? Do you need help finding her? Should we go call someone?"

Pausing, Lisa's shoulders go rigid before she slowly turns back to face the four kids. Sam notices gold stitching on the front of her shirt that's caught in a ray of sunlight as she twists. Even from this distance, she recognizes the same odd diagram that was on the paper in the boat. Briefly distracted, Sam almost misses the raw terror that flashes in Lisa's eyes.

"*What* are you talking about?" Lisa says evenly, her eyes darting back and forth among them.

"Erica thought Sam was Carrie," Ally explains, spreading her arms wide in a non-threatening gesture. "She told us that she was trying to find her sister."

Lisa lets out a big sigh. Was it relief? Hesitating, she looks fleetingly at Erica before seeming to make up her mind.

"You were already told that Erica has…problems. She made it up. There's no one named Carrie, and we *don't* need your help!" Without another word, she yanks at Erica's hand and then heads back down the trail at a brisk pace.

"But-" Sam persists, before a hand on her arm stops her.

"She obviously doesn't want to talk to us, Sam," Ally tells her. "Just let her go."

"Yeah," Hunter agrees. "She didn't even thank us for risking our lives to help her!"

Remembering the green, troubling eyes that first greeted her, Sam isn't convinced. "There's something wrong here," she tries to explain, shaking her head.

"Wrong in her head, you mean," John counters. "Look, Sam, we offered to help her and she clearly doesn't want it. For whatever reason, that woman put herself *and* her little girl in a really dangerous situation. We shouldn't get involved. We'll tell your folks what happened when we get back, and let them decide what to do."

Sam knows that John is right, but there's still something nagging at her. Something she should remember.

"I think we need to go back now," Ally suggests. "It's not like we can go any farther."

No one disagrees, and they all file back the way they came, each lost in thought. They haven't gone very far when Sam, who's in the lead, stops dead in her tracks, causing Ally to walk right into her. Hunter starts to laugh at them, but stops when he sees the serious look on his sister's face.

"What is it?" he asks, glancing briefly into the shadowy woods.

"Erica wasn't lying!" Sam blurts out. Seeing her friend's confused expressions, she rushes to explain. "There's really *is* someone named Carrie, and I think she might need our help!"

12

"I think that's a pretty big stretch, Sam."

John is leaning against the trunk of a huge cedar tree, his arms crossed over his chest. Ally and Hunter are sharing a stump, and all of them have been listening to Sam explain about the backpack and papers she had seen while on the boat.

"What?" Sam demands, frustrated. "There's a girls backpack with the name Carrie on the phone clipped to it, on the boat that Erica's *dad* was on! Don't you think that's a huge coincidence?"

Sam had nearly forgotten about the bag. She hadn't even said anything about it to Ally yesterday. Compared to the confrontation with the men on the boat, and fear of getting into trouble, it simply didn't seem important.

"And what about that logo thing Sam told us about?" Ally presses, turning to look at her brother. "If the same one is on Lisa's shirt, don't you think that proves that she's connected to the boat, too? Erica mistook Sam for this girl, Carrie, so the backpack would be something Sam might have. That means the girl would be around our age."

"So what exactly do you want to do about it?" Hunter asks, annoyed. "Because as soon as you explain *how* you saw that backpack, Mom and Dad are going to stop listening. You're going to get us *all* sent home, and I'm actually having a good time here. I'd like to still be around on Friday for the sand castle festival. If that lady wants to run around in the woods with her crazy kid, then let her. It's none of our business!"

All four of them start talking at once, debating both sides of the argument. Sam regrets having shared the encounter on the boat with her brother. She should have known that he'd try to use it against her! "Well, I'm sure that Dad would be thrilled to find out about your midnight swim!" she blurts out at an opportune moment, and then immediately wishes she could take it back when she sees the look on John's face.

Throwing his hands in the air, John pushes away from the tree to stand his full six feet before bellowing at them all to stop. It has the desired effect. "We're *all* right," he says reasonably. "I agree that the backpack makes the whole thing with Lisa and Erica seem suspicious. Also, that the company shirt that Lisa was wearing might tie her into whatever her husband is doing with those weird foreign guys. But that doesn't change the fact that our only option right now would be to go to your parents and call Lisa a liar, based on something that Sam saw while sneaking onto a strangers boat without permission. Even if they were able to see past that and listen to us, what could they do? Go over to their house and accuse them of…what? Don't you see? There's nothing to accuse them *of*. To even t*alk* to them about it, would be admitting to trespassing, which really *is* something you could legally get in trouble for."

Now that John has broken it all down, Sam is feeling pretty stupid. Thank goodness he was with them so that she didn't make the huge mistake of running to her parents. He's absolutely right; the only thing that would happen, is that *she* would get into trouble. That would mean that Carrie would still be lost, and they wouldn't be able to help her.

"So now what?" Ally asks quietly, after a long moment of silence.

"Stick with the original plan, and tell my parents exactly what happened out here," Sam states with a new resolve. "But we'll be sure to keep an eye out for any clues about this girl Carrie, and maybe try to figure out what kind of business they're involved in."

Smiling, Ally is glad to see Sam's confidence returning. She really is quite smart, and can come up with some amazing ideas.

"How do you plan to do that, Sherlock?" Hunter's smart remark cuts into her thoughts, making Ally frown at him.

"The way we *always* do it," Sam says without hesitation. Looking at Ally, she gives her friend a big wink. "By paying attention."

***

Sitting in the window of a small ice cream shop, Sam looks out at the throng of tourists walking by. Even though it's nearly nine o'clock at night, it's still busy. The boys had agreed to the movies, which they just got out of, and her dad was happy to let them take the van.

Earlier, Ethan and Kathy Wolf had sat and listened in amazement to the story that the kids told them. When they had finished, they were clearly disturbed by it, but not angry. The girls had done what they were told by not going on the trail alone, and they had all helped someone who obviously needed it. They immediately went next door to check on Lisa and Erica, but no one answered.

"I'll go over tomorrow and visit with Lisa," Kathy assured them. "Don't worry. I'll make sure they're okay, and maybe I can put her in touch with some resources for getting help with Erica. I still have several contacts at the state level for various programs."

Disappointed that her parents had failed to focus on the whole 'lost sister' issue, Sam couldn't blame them. They didn't have a reason to, since they believed Lisa's explanation that Erica just made it up. Content that her mom would at least talk to Lisa, she had to let it go. Well...with her parents, anyway.

Now, Sam concentrates on the people walking by, but she hasn't seen the men from the boat, the old man who told them the Captain Wood story, or any young girls that look like her.

Turning her attention back to the conversation at their table, she has to laugh. Hunter and Ally have been discussing the ending to the movie for a grueling fifteen minutes now. It was a cliffhanger and they have differing ideas as to what it meant.

"She clearly got away!" Ally insists, her ice cream dripping down her hand, forgotten. "That's why they're already making a second movie, Hunter."

"No," Hunter rallies. "The crystal skull was activated and transported *all* of them! So they-"

"Did you read the books?" John

interrupts. When both Hunter and Ally look at him with blank stares, he laughs. "Because I did, and I know what happens in the next movie. But I'm not going to tell you," he continues, obviously enjoying the frustration he's causing. "So you'll either have to wait until next year, or...you can borrow the trilogy from me!"

Shaking her head at the new round of bickering this causes, Sam turns to look back out the large window...and freezes. Directly across the street, Kevin Moore has just stepped away from the post office. *There must be post office boxes there,* Sam thinks. Their own small town has the same set-up. The little room is basically a wall of small, locked mailboxes, and can be accessed by the owner anytime. Sam imagines the people who live on the boats must get their mail this way.

Elbowing Ally, who's seated next to her, Sam points towards Mr. Moore silently. They watch as he rips open a large envelope, pulls out a small, bubble-wrapped item, and then tosses the paper into a wastebasket before walking away.

Once he's out of sight, Sam nudges Ally to scoot over so that she can get out of the seat. "Wait here," she says quietly.

The boys don't have a chance to ask her what she's doing before Sam is out the door and running across the street. They watch in confusion as she walks pointedly to the open-topped garbage can and reaches in.

In less than a minute, Sam is back inside, re-joining them at the table. Her face is flushed, and she's clearly excited about something. "Our next clue," she announces matter-of-factly, setting a large brown envelope on the table.

The three other kids all lean forward to get a clear look at the distinct logo in the top corner, in the return address space.

"That's a double-helix," John says with certainty. "Well, sort of. It's a drawing *based* on the double-helix. That's DNA," he explains to the others.

"I remember now!" Sam exclaims. "We studied that in our science class last year. I knew I had seen it somewhere. But yeah, it's not exactly like it, which is what threw me off. What's the company name next to it?"

"BioCore Resources," Hunter reads. Under the heading, the double-helix design blends into the M and W above and below it, which then spell out 'Meckling and Wesseler Enterprises.'

"There's no address," Sam notes, both intrigued and disappointed.

"It's a *bioengineering* company in Denmark," Ally announces, and they all look at her in surprise. Holding her phone up, she shrugs. "They've got Wi-Fi here," she explains happily.

"Let me see that," John asks, taking the phone from his sister. Reading intently for several minutes, he finally looks up, brows furrowed. "It's some sort of research facility, but most of their contracts are with governments and aren't publicized," he summarizes.

After that bit of interesting information sinks in, they sit looking at each other for a moment before Sam breaks the silence.

"Well," she whispers, looking around the store with a new sense of danger. "This all just got a whole lot weirder."

13

MOVING SHADOWS

After several more searches on the internet, Sam, Ally, and their two brothers still lack information. They try rearranging words, and also try adding Lisa and Kevin's names, but without results.

"*If* those are even their real names," Sam ponders, feeling a bit defeated.

"Don't you think you might be making this into something bigger than it is?" Hunter complains, working on his second sundae. "Maybe they really *are* just on vacation, and have a kid that likes to run off and make stuff up."

"Then why would Mr. Moore be meeting

up with those foreign men on the boat?" Ally points out. "I bet those guys are from Denmark. There was company stuff all over the inside of that boat."

Shrugging, Hunter licks the last of the hot fudge from his spoon. "I dunno. Maybe the guy is important and his business partners needed something from him. Who cares?"

Drumming her fingers on the table, Sam considers her brothers comments. "Sometimes," she explains, "you need to just follow your gut. There's something wrong here, and I think that the backpack is a key to it all."

Rolling his eyes, Hunter looks to John for support. To his surprise, the older boy is nodding in agreement with Sam.

"Hunter, your dad invited us to the marina tomorrow. I think we should go, and try to find the boat. We won't go inside, of course," he says pointedly to Sam, with a smirk. "But we can snoop around it, and look in the windows if no one is there. Maybe we can find out if there's been a girl seen on it."

"And then what?" Hunter continues his campaign against their investigation. "What are we gonna do if we find something?"

"If we can get enough evidence that there's some sort of foul play, we'll share it with my parents and let them go to the authorities," Sam says with conviction.

Coming from another twelve-year-old, this might seem like a ridiculous plan. But this isn't just any twelve-year-old. This is Samantha Wolf, who has a knack for finding…and solving mysteries.

They make it back to the beach house just before their ten o'clock curfew, the envelope safely folded and tucked in Sam's back pocket. Ally had been wary of holding onto it, but John reminded them that it was thrown out in a public garbage can, making it okay to keep.

Sam finds herself lying in bed a couple of hours later, reading the words on the envelope for the hundredth time. The sender didn't put down the name of the recipient, only the post office box number and town. Very cryptic.

Rubbing her eyes, Sam wishes she could fall asleep, but there are too many thoughts racing through her mind. Is there really a missing girl named Carrie? What were Lisa and Erica doing in the woods today? What kind of work does Kevin do for a secret bioengineering company? And why are those men on the boat here?

Finally giving up on sleep, Sam rolls out of bed. Checking first to make sure Ally is actually asleep, she then tiptoes to the French doors. Before she can pull them open, there's a light knock on the bedroom door. Jumping, she turns in time to see Hunter let himself in.

"Can't sleep?" She whispers when he joins her at the entrance to the balcony.

"Nah," he mumbles. "Figured I'd come check things out. See if that crazy sound was out here again."

Smiling as they step outside, Sam realizes she and Hunter might be more alike than either of them would ever admit. Glancing sideways at her brother, she can barely make out his form as he leans against the banister. Sam suspects that his criticism earlier wasn't all that sincere.

"No fog," he observes.

He's right. There isn't a hint of the thick condensation that blanketed the beach the past two nights. But the moon hasn't risen above the

Olympic Mountains behind them yet, so it's still nearly impossible to see anything.

Peering in the general area Sam thinks the lighthouse should be, she doesn't see any sign of the light, either. Disappointed, her eyes drift to the dark beach. The water, sand, and woods all blend together in the inky blackness.

Wait. *What was that?*

Straining to focus on an area where Sam thinks she saw movement, she can't be sure if her eyes are playing tricks on her or not.

No, she's definitely not imagining it. There's someone running on the beach! The shadow dances in and out of focus, far down at the other end of the cove.

"Hunter!" Sam shouts, not daring to look away.

"What? I don't see any floating candles up in your lighthouse."

"No! There's someone down on the beach!"

The lone shadow is joined by two other, bigger ones. Sam watches as they weave around each other, then a spray of water erupts near them, and when Sam tries to re-focus on them, they're gone! Wishing for some moonlight, she waits to see if they reappear, but it's just too dark. She's lost them.

"I don't see anything," Hunter replies. "I'm going to bed."

"Wait! Don't you think it's odd that someone is down there this late?"

"Not really. John and I were doing the same thing a couple of nights ago, remember?" Hunter's teeth flash in the dark as he smiles before turning and opening the door. "I dunno if you're right about any of this," he adds, pausing. "But if you are, I hope we can help figure it out."

He's gone before Sam can answer, but she doesn't need to. Thankful to have her brother and John here, she turns back to study the beach again. *Is there some mystical creature out there?* she wonders, a cool breeze working its way through her nightgown. *Or do we need to worry more about the people next door?*

14

CLUES AND ACCUSATIONS

Although Sam didn't get much sleep the night before, she's still the first one up, eager to go examine the beach. It's a very low tide this morning, but it's quickly coming back in. Any clues as to who was out there last night could be washed away soon.

It takes a full five minutes of pushing and pulling to coax Ally out of bed. Sam almost leaves without her, but Ally finally stumbles into her shorts, still half-asleep.

"I don't understand why you think we'll

find something useful," Ally yawns after Sam explains what happened the night before. Pulling on a matching tank top, Ally throws her messy hair up in a loose bun. "You don't even know for sure that you saw someone."

Ignoring her complaints, Sam takes Ally by the shoulders. "We're collecting sea shells," she whispers, steering her out of the room and through the silent house.

They pass Sam's mom, who just sat down in one of the big wicker chairs in the family room with a steaming cup of coffee. The early morning hours are often her only free time from the twins, other than when they take naps.

"You should take a bag!" Kathy calls after them as they scoot past her. "You might find a conch shell with the water this low!"

Although Sam's family lives near the ocean, it's in a part of the Puget Sound. The tide rises and falls, of course, but when it retreats, it leaves behind huge beds of mud. It's nearly impossible to do anything there other than dig for clams. It's a treat to be out near the open ocean now, with bigger waves and nice sand to search for shells.

"Thanks, Mom!" Sam says, turning back to grab a plastic grocery sack off the kitchen counter. "We won't be too long. I'll help feed Tabby and Addy when we get back."

Her mom grimaces at her use of the nicknames, but doesn't comment. Sam's parents have a thing with naming them after their grandparents. That's fine, except for the fact that the names are very formal. Sam insists on going by the shorter version of her own name, but usually respects her mom's wishes for calling the twins by their proper ones. Unless, such as now, she's in a hurry and doesn't have time to protest. Besides, she thinks the rhyming names are cute.

Over half an hour later, they reach the general area where Sam thought she saw the shadows. They could have gotten there sooner, but ornate shells, littering the ground. distracted them. With their bag half full, they make their way along the empty stretch of beach. They've only encountered a handful of people, in spite of the prime beachcombing conditions. The tide is swiftly coming in now, causing Sam to rush Ally along.

"Okay, so now what?" Ally questions,

jumping forward when a particularly large wave nips at her heels. The morning is still cool and she doesn't want to get wet.

Unsure how to answer, Sam walks a bit farther before throwing her hands up in frustration and turning back to her friend.

"I don't know, Ally! I guess that maybe I'm being stupid for thinking we might actually find something. Like they're going to leave us a sign or something that says 'look here.'"

"What about 'help?'" Ally says excitedly.

"Huh?"

"No! I mean a sign that says 'help'!" Ally explains, still not making any sense. When Sam just stares at her, she rolls her eyes and points behind her. "Look!"

Following Ally's outstretched hand, Sam searches the sand near her feet and then gasps in surprise. Sure enough, scrawled into the sand are big capital letters: H E L P.

"Oh my gosh!" she shouts. "This had to have been made by whoever I saw last night. We got out here right after sunrise and there wasn't *anyone* out this far."

"Or else it was written earlier in the day

yesterday," Ally suggests, studying the words.

Watching the water wash away the lower end of the P, Sam straightens up abruptly. "No. It *had* to have been last night. The tide didn't go out until well after dark. This was under water until then...like it's going to be again in just a little bit," she adds, realizing that the evidence is being rapidly erased. "There's no way to go get my mom and show her before it's gone!" she moans, wishing they had gotten out here sooner.

As a new wave bubbles up to the bottom edge of the E, Ally shouts at Sam to step back. "I can take a picture of it!" she tells her, producing the ever-present cell phone from her back pocket.

Relieved to have a way to preserve the message, Sam looks around for anything else suspicious while Ally gets several shots of it. Coming up empty-handed, Sam joins Ally in watching the last of the letters get reclaimed by the ocean. With nothing more to do, they head back to the beach house.

Sam can tell right away that something is wrong when they approach the deck where her mom is standing, obviously waiting for them.

She's got her arms crossed and a troubled expression clouds her face. "I need to have a talk with you, girls," she says, her tone serious.

Glancing uneasily at each other, Sam and Ally climb the stairs and leave the smelly bag of shells outside, then follow Kathy into the family room. The house is quiet, and Sam figures her dad and the boys have already left for the marina, and the twins are sleeping in.

Did Mr. Moore or the harbormaster make a complaint about us? Sam wonders, the all too familiar feeling of guilt welling up inside her.

"Lisa Moore saw me outside drinking my coffee, and came over to speak with me," Sam's mother begins, eyeing them both closely. When neither girl says anything, she continues. "Her version of the story is much different than yours. Apparently, she and Erica saw you two enter the woods earlier in the day and *that's* what compelled her to create the story of a lost sister that looked like you, Sam. Well, that and a cartoon she had just watched. She tends to confuse reality and make-believe, I guess."

Sam is trying to digest what her mom just said. "Wait," she cries in alarm. "Lisa told you that she saw us go into the woods *before* them? That's a lie!"

Holding up a hand, Kathy stops the expected tirade. "Let me finish," she says evenly, leaving no room for discussion. "Shortly after watching you disappeared onto the trail, Erica snuck out when she was supposed to be down for a nap. Lisa finally found her a short distance into the woods, after locating a dropped hairband near the trailhead. It was a nice walk, so she decided to explore it further with Erica. That was when she slipped. She wants to thank for helping her. However," Kathy continues, "she also made it clear that she has no interest in speaking further with me, or in having you two around Erica."

"Mom, she's lying about seeing us *and* she's totally downplaying what happened. She didn't just 'slip.' She almost died!"

"I know, Sam. I already spoke with the boys about it and they swear that you two were on the beach the whole time and that they *followed* you to the trail, and then had to talk you into going on the hike. They confirmed that Erica and Lisa had to have gone in there quite some time before the rest of you. I have no idea why she would bend the truth like this, but I think it best that we all steer clear of them from now on. Understand?"

Hesitating, Sam looks at Ally seated silently beside her, firmly gripping her phone, the picture of the word 'help' still lit up on the screen.

"But what if Erica *wasn't* making it all up?" she asks cautiously, peering sideways at her mom.

"Sam...," Kathy says firmly. "Do *not* start. I mean it. While Lisa's response to her daughter's problems is troubling, I won't let you turn this into something it's not."

"Shouldn't we at least consider the possibility that Carrie might be real? Or that she could need our help?" Glancing back at the phone, Sam watches the picture go dark, perhaps a sign that now isn't the time to bring it up.

Kathy covers her face with her hands, and speaks through her fingers. "No. We shouldn't, Sam." She utters the words tiredly, rather than with anger. Coming to what appears to be a hard decision, she slides her hands up through her hair before leveling both girls with a hard stare. "Your father and I talked about this before he left for the day. We both agree that we made it clear before coming here that we weren't going to put up with any…unacceptable behavior. You aren't going to get another warning about this. Push the issue, and I'm taking you home."

Sam watches Ally slowly put the phone with the incriminating photo back into her pocket. Swallowing hard, Sam reaches for her friend's hand and gives it a reassuring squeeze.

"Okay, Mom." Forcing the expected answer, she hopes it sounds sincere. It's clear now that they're on their own.

15

MAYBE BROTHERS AREN'T SO BAD AFTER ALL

John stands in a wide stance on the dock, shading his eyes in order to get a good look at the suspicious boat. He and Hunter have just completed the guided tour of the larger fishing vessel with Ethan. It didn't last nearly as long as the same tour did with Sam and Ally, who asked a ton of questions. While he enjoys boats and all, he just isn't that interested in how every little thing on them works.

What he *is* interested in is getting closer to

their current target. They've cautiously circled around the marina from a distance, making sure there isn't any obvious activity onboard the boat in question. They haven't seen anyone come or go, but there could still be someone inside.

They can't afford to have Mr. Moore or the other thugs complain about them. Sam and Hunter's parents are already on edge after Lisa Moore came over, giving her lame excuse and lies. John understands *why* they want to stay out of it, and not get involved…but to be honest, he's beginning to see how Sam and his sister get themselves caught up in this stuff. It's kinda exciting. Hunter, on the other hand, doesn't appear to share his enthusiasm.

"Can we get outta here now?" Hunter says earnestly, looking over his shoulder for the third time. "It's not like we're going to be able to learn anything that could help. This is stupid."

Ignoring him, John silently approaches the bow and tries to read the name painted boldly across the front. "Her Vaere Drager. I wonder what *that* means," he mumbles under his breath.

"I'm going to peek in the window real quick," John tells Hunter, deciding to look the name up later. Unaware how closely he's mimicking Sam, he moves towards the nearest portal. Before Hunter can object, John leans out and cups his hands to either side of the small, round glass.

It's dark inside, but he can still make out the room. It's very close to how Sam described it, except that the table is cleared of everything but a torn sheet of bubble wrap. There's no sign of the laptops, paper, or backpack. Disappointed, he pushes away from the boat and then crosses his arms over his chest, thinking about the situation.

"Well?" Hunter asks impatiently. "What'd you see?"

"Not much," John says quietly as he turns away abruptly. Making his way along the length of the boat, he looks around again, then peers into the last window on the exposed side.

The view through the porthole is partially blocked by a curtain, but he can still see beyond it, into a small bedroom. The bed is unmade and there are towels and blankets strewn across the floor...and in the far corner, a backpack. A tie-dyed backpack with what looks like a phone case hanging off it. It's too dark to see any writing on it, but he's certain it's the same one Sam tripped over.

"Bingo!" John says triumphantly, but then frowns again when he turns to Hunter. "I can see the backpack your sister told us about, but that's pretty much it. No one's in there, and there's no real evidence someone is staying there, just a bunch of towels and blankets.

"Whatchya doin'?" A small voice behind them makes the boys jump. They both stumble guiltily away from the boat.

Hunter's convinced he's about to have a heart attack, but then breaks out laughing when he sees their accuser. Hardly more than three feet tall, the small boy has a head full of tight, blonde curls. His vivid blue eyes are wide and sparkling with curiosity. Wiping at his runny nose with a small fist, he continues to look back and forth between the older boys, seemingly unoffended by the laughter.

"We're just admiring this cool boat," John says politely, squatting down so that he's eye level with the little boy. "My name is John, what's yours?"

"Bucky," he says happily, rocking back on

his heels. "My momma says it's not polite to look in people's windows," he adds in a hushed voice. "But don't worry, I won't tell no one."

Chuckling, John glances at Hunter and raises his eyebrows. "Thanks, Bucky," he says, turning back to him. "I'm wondering if you've ever seen a girl on this boat. Her name is Carrie."

Scrunching up his nose so tight that John thinks it must hurt, Bucky shakes his head dramatically. "Nope! Just those mean guys who yelled at me." He hugs himself at the memory. "Told me to mind my own business. Pappa says I gotta stay away from them. They don't act normal. They wake me up almost every night, 'cause they go someplace late and don't come back sometimes until I'm eating breakfast. They're weird."

Not convinced that Bucky ever took a breath while he was talking, John breaks into a wide smile. This is good stuff.

"That *is* weird, Bucky. They ever have anyone with them?"

"Nah...I just only seen the four of them."

"Four?" Hunter echoes, sharing a surprised look with John. It's safe to assume that the third guy would be Kevin Moore, but what about the fourth? "Are you sure?"

"Uh-huh," Bucky drawls. "I know how many four is. I can count to ten! They all talk real funny, except for the one 'merican. Momma says it's 'cause they're from a different... umm...whatchya call those places?"

"A different country?" John suggests good-naturedly.

"Yeah! That's it. A different country. I still think they're mean, though. I don't care if it's 'cause they're from....umm...someplace else."

"Bucky!" a voice calls sharply. Looking for the source, John finds a young woman standing in the bow of the boat that's docked next to Her Vare Drager. "Come back here and stop bothering those young men."

"Bye!" Bucky says cheerfully, obviously used to being called away from strangers. He's skipping across the dock before either boy has a chance to say goodbye.

Standing up, John suddenly finds himself as eager as Hunter to put some distance between themselves and this place. Mr. Wolf was happy to let them take the van, so they didn't have to stay at the marina all day. They just have to come back later to pick him up.

"Let's go get some lunch at the restaurant before going back to the house," John says. "I'll bet there's Wi-Fi in there that we can use."

"Why do we need Wi-Fi?" Hunter asks, already making his way back towards the buildings.

"Because I've got my tablet. I brought it to read books on, but I can use it to search for some more info on this bioengineering company. The search function is a lot easier to use than the one on Ally's phone. Plus, we can try and figure out what the name of the boat means."

"Why does that matter?" Hunter wants to know. They've stopped in the shadow of the restaurant, and can finally face each other without being blinded by the harsh sunlight.

"The name chosen for a boat usually holds some form of significance," John explains. "You should know that, Hunter. Hasn't your dad talked about it?"

Shrugging, Hunter looks a bit chastised. "Probably. I guess I don't always pay attention."

"Well, I read about it a couple years ago.

And if these guys *are* from Denmark, then it's probably even more likely. I think that your sister might be right," he continues, the change in subject catching Hunter off guard.

"Right about what?" Hunter wants to know.

"That something isn't right here." A lone cry of a bald eagle circling overhead pierces the air, adding a sense of urgency to the observation. "We need to figure out what it is."

16

HERE BE DRAGONS

"Here Be Dragons. What does that mean?" Ally asks her brother. "And how did you figure it out?"

The four of them are gathered in the back of the house, in the boys' room, under the guise of playing video games. After sharing their encounter with Bucky, and what they did and did not see inside the boat, the boys then explained their findings on the name.

"Well, first I just tried a search for the name, but that didn't lead anywhere," John tells her. "Then, I figured that since the company is based in Denmark, that I should try a translation using the common language there, which turns out to be Danish. It was easy then to just plug it into the online program."

"Very smart," Sam says approvingly, just a little bit disappointed that she hadn't been in on it. "I know I've heard that before, but I can't remember where."

"It's been used in lots of things," John confirms. "But the original meaning was on old maps."

"Old maps?" Ally questions. "What kind of maps?"

"It goes back to medieval times," John tells them. "It means that it's dangerous or unexplored territory. On some of the oldest maps recovered, they put the pictures of dragons and sea serpents in the regions that were unknown, as a warning."

"So these guys like to *brag* about being dangerous." Hunter has been pretending to be engrossed in the video game he's playing, but Sam knows that he's just as interested as the rest of them. Putting the controller down now, he turns around to look at them. "Doesn't that bother any of you?"

"I'm not convinced that's why they chose it," Sam counters, not really answering her brother's question. When he raises his eyebrows at her, she searches for the best way to explain her thoughts. "I think we're missing the bigger picture here," she finally states, including John and Ally in her observation. "John, you said you found out some more stuff about BioCore Resources?"

"Yeah...," he confirms, pulling out a folded napkin from his back pocket. It was the only thing available to write on at the restaurant.

"It was a lot easier to try some different searches with my tablet, and the Wi-Fi was much faster there than in that ice cream shop. It isn't much, but aside from the secret government contracts, they also manufacture vaccines for WHO, the World Health Organization. I only found that out because of an article on the company's CEO, or Chief Executive Officer. He's part of a special vaccine board for the non-profit group, and has been active in some programs going into poorer countries. There was a scandal last year, where he was accused of having some ulterior motives. That rather than being a humanitarian, he was using the people as guinea pigs.

"Apparently, one of the biggest hang-ups in producing vaccines, or any sort of medicine, is getting to the point of doing human trials. Especially in the developed countries, where they make the people who create it jump through a bunch of hoops before allowing them to test it out on real people. He got around that by being put in charge of this program, and then sending out his own unfinished vaccines to the un-monitored countries. They tested it on unsuspecting people, improved it, and then turned around and sold it for a profit of billions of dollars."

"How could they get away with that?" Ally demands, arms crossed angrily.

"They shouldn't have, but they did," John replies. "They're smart, and knew exactly what they were doing. While it was unethical and wrong, nothing they did was illegal. At least, not in the countries they were doing it in. Some of the claims couldn't be proven, so it never went anywhere legally. I guess the big pharmaceutical companies don't care, because they keep buying their stuff. It's all about the money. But…I found some other things, too. It's a bit more controversial. One doctor over in Africa wrote a paper claiming that BioCore wasn't just testing vaccines. He believed that they were creating something much more dangerous. I only found the one article though, and then nothing else."

Nodding her head as if expecting it, Sam claps her hands together. "That's it!" she exclaims, "*That's* what the name on the boat means!"

"Sam, what are you talking about?" Hunter asks in frustration. Sometimes he just can't figure out how his sister's brain works, and it drives him crazy.

"It isn't because the people in the *boat* are dangerous," she says, unfazed by her brothers tone. "It means that the kind of work the *company* does is dangerous and uncharted. What if the vaccine or drug, or whatever it is they're creating, is something never seen before and considered dangerous?" Sam asks, her eyes wide. "Kevin and Lisa must both work for this company. But *why* are they here in Wood's Cove? And I have *no* idea why Erica and her missing sister, Carrie, would be involved," she adds, a bit deflated.

"Whoa…," John says, holding his hands out defensively and grinning. "We might be getting ahead of ourselves here. I admit that this new info makes this company a lot more suspicious, but there's a good chance that it doesn't have anything to do with what's going on here. Heck, we don't even know if those rumors are true!"

"But what about the missing, fourth man that Bucky saw?" Sam presses, refusing to let it go. "And the late nightly trips that the boat makes? They have to be going to the lighthouse! I'll bet that the light I've seen is from them."

"That's *another* big leap to make," John says, his frown deepening. "We've never even seen a boat out there!"

"Well, I think that Sam is right about the boat's name," Ally says, coming to her friend's defense. "And there's enough evidence to link it, Kevin, and those other guys to BioCore Resources. Since they only do secret work for governments, and make vaccines, and they're getting stuff mailed to them here from the company in Denmark, then it's safe to assume that they're up to something."

"Or they could be on vacation," Hunter suggests, back to playing his game. "I'm sure that even mad scientists have to take a break sometime."

In spite of wanting to be mad at Hunter's lack of enthusiasm, Sam laughs. He could very well be right. But that little nagging voice in the back of her head won't allow her to believe it.

***

Once again, it's a fogless night. The four of them are huddled on the small deck, patiently watching the dark ocean for any signs of the gathering mist. They've been out there for over half an hour already, and Sam is cold, tired, and very frustrated.

"Can we go back inside now?" Hunter asks, visibly shivering.

Gripping the railing tightly, Sam leans back from it and gazes up at the endless twinkling stars above them. *Maybe Hunter is right,* she thinks forlornly. *I might be trying too hard this time to find a mystery where there really isn't one.*

"There obviously isn't going to be any fog," John observes. "I vote we go to bed before your mom and dad discover we aren't in our rooms, and come yell at us."

The two boys begin their retreat as Sam pulls herself back up to look in the direction of the lighthouse. "Wait!" she cries. "Look at the lighthouse!"

Joining her again, they strain to see what she's all excited about. Sure enough, in the distance is a weak light, clearly visible above the cliffs. As they watch, it blinks out and then back again.

"Odd," John murmurs, more to himself than anyone else.

The light continues to flicker, and it's quickly apparent that it's a consistent pattern.

"Why is it doing that?" Ally asks, both confused and enthralled at the same time.

"It wasn't doing that the last time I saw it," Sam tells her friends. "What do you think it means?"

"That someone is using a cheap candle?"

Hunter suggests, always the comic.

"It's Morse code!" John exclaims, tapping out the rhythm on the bannister. "Three quick flashes, three slow ones, and then three fast ones again: SOS. It's the universal message for distress!"

He's right, Sam realizes, as she watches the message repeat one more time. "How in the world do you know that?"

"Scouts," John replies. "It's pretty much standard learning for any kind of survival training."

"What are we going to do?" Ally demands, more concerned with how to handle the distress call.

"We've got to go get my parents," Sam says without hesitation. "Then they'll *have* to believe us!"

"Good luck with that," Hunter says flatly.

"Why do you always have to be so negative?" Sam questions, going to the door. "Can't you just agree with me for once?"

"I'd love to, but I don't think our parents are going to believe anything, because now the light stopped."

Her hopes crashing, Sam spins back and searches frantically for the flashing message….but Hunter is right, it's gone. Dejected, she flops down on one of the two folding chairs, and covers her face with her hands. "They'll never believe it," she says, her voice muffled. "If I go in there and try to convince them that somehow there is a girl name Carrie in the lighthouse signaling us for help…I'll be going home in the morning." Looking up, she struggles to see their faces in the faint starlight. "And then no one will help Carrie, or whoever it is that's out there!"

"Then we have to go there ourselves," Ally says with surprising resolve. Normally, she's the one who needs to be persuaded to do anything dangerous or against the rules.

"How?" Hunter asks. "The trail is gone. Plus, we don't even know that the signal is real. I mean, it could just be some kids that think it's funny….you know, scare the tourists with the whole 'ghost in the tower' thing."

"The only way we can know for sure is to check," Sam says. "At least get close enough to hear any calls for help. I promise to let it go if we don't find her there, ok?"

Hunter and John lean towards each other and talk quietly for a moment, before turning back to Sam and Ally.

"Okay," John agrees. "But only if it isn't dangerous, and we can do it during the day, without lying about it."

"The old man who told us the story said that there's a way to get there by boat," Sam answers, her spirits already lifting. "We just have to go back, find him, and convince him to tell us how."

17

CAPTAIN BROWN

The next morning, they are in Wood's Cove before nine a.m. They didn't even have to come up with an excuse. Turns out, they have to pre-register for the sand castle contest happening early that afternoon, and the booth is in the town center.

After standing in line briefly with some sunburned tourists with cheap gift-shop sand buckets, they sign up, then slowly wander around the boardwalk in front of the stores.

Sam bites nervously at her already short nails, worrying that the old man won't show up.

After forty minutes, they are all hot and getting hungry. This is the first time that Sam hasn't been sure about what to do. With their other mysteries, it's always been so clear.

It's hard to believe that it's already Friday. So not only does Sam feel time slipping away because of the distress call last night...but they have to go home in a couple of days. Groaning in frustration, she wipes the sweat off her forehead and flops down on a bench.

"You're looking like you lost your best friend there, missy." Leaping to her feet, Sam spins around eagerly to face the man she's been searching for. He's wearing the same dirty clothes as before. Leaning against a lamp post, he has the unlit pipe sticking out of his mouth, bobbing up and down in time to his laughter.

"Ally!" Sam calls out, without looking around for her friend. She's afraid the old storyteller will disappear if she turns away. Ally, John, and Hunter are soon beside her. As she goes to introduce them, Sam realizes she doesn't even know the man's name.

"Captain Brown, at your service," he announces when asked, with the typical dramatic flair the girls have grown accustomed to. "One of the last *real* sea captains left in this town," he adds somewhat grudgingly.

"It's an honor to meet you, sir," John says politely, shaking the man's old, weathered hand. "My name is John Parker. You've already met my sister, Allyson. This here is Hunter Wolf, Sam's brother."

Turning his attention to Hunter, Captain Brown scrutinizes him for some time before breaking out in a fresh smile. "Hello, lad. Did you come to hear the Wood's Cove story?" he asks a bit eagerly.

"Actually," Sam interrupts, stepping around the bench so she can stand next to the captain. "We were looking for you for another reason."

Raising his bushy eyebrows questioningly, Captain Brown tilts his grizzled head and looks at each of them in turn. "What other purpose could you possibly have for an old captain?" he asks suspiciously, pulling absently at his long beard.

"We're hoping you can tell us how to get to the lighthouse," Sam explains. "You said before that you can get there by boat. I figure there must be a special place to go, because the whole thing looks like a cliff."

Already shaking his head, Captain Brown spits out his pipe and waves it at them earnestly. "I told you before that the place is dangerous!" he barks. "Besides, I haven't used my rowboat for years and you two girls have no business trying to handle it."

"A rowboat?" Ally repeats, looking at Sam with a smile.

"But we won't be by ourselves!" Sam rushes to say, making a note of Ally's observation. "Our brothers would be with us. My parents won't allow us on the trails without them."

"I can handle just about any rowboat, sir," John adds convincingly.

"And we aren't going to go *inside* the lighthouse," Sam continues when the older man seems to hesitate. "We're just looking for something fun to do this afternoon, and thought it would be neat to see it up close."

"You boys would be with them?" Captain Brown finally asks, after drumming his chin thoughtfully for a full minute.

When John and Hunter nod in response, the old man lets out a deep sigh, coming to a decision.

"About a mile up the trail that starts at the beach, there's a smaller path that veers down towards the water. You have to watch for it, because it hasn't been used in a long time. It's marked by a large tree that was struck by lightning over twenty years ago."

"Oh, I remember seeing that!" Sam shouts. "We've been on the main trail already."

"Don't interrupt me, child. I'll forget what I was saying."

Sam apologizes and then has to wait another minute while the captain gathers his thoughts together again.

"That trail ends at a small, hidden cove. It's flooded when the tide is up, but nearly dry when it's out. That's when you have to go…at low tide. It's the only way that you can get to the lighthouse. Stay close to shore, just beyond the breakers. When you see two tall rocks shaped like triangles touching at the top, that's where you need to go. These are under water at high tide, but when it's low, you can pass right through them, like a tunnel. Beyond them is a protected spot to pull the boat up and go to shore. The trail leading up is steep and rocky, so be cautious. You mustn't stay once the tide turns, or you'll be stuck. Do you understand that? Because I won't be held responsible for any foolishness on your part."

"We promise that we'll be careful!" Sam assures him, trying not to sound too excited. "And we'll take good care of your boat."

"It's not the boat I'm concerned about," he mumbles, already shuffling away. "Beware of Wood's Sea Creature!" he adds over his shoulder. "He's always watching his cove."

***

The Sand Castle Festival is a grand affair, with everything from cotton candy vendors, to paragliding rides off jet skis. Although they begged their parents endlessly, Sam and Hunter were forced to watch the daredevils, rather than participate.

"You couldn't pay me to do that!" Ally

gasps as yet another person is hauled into the air like a kite. The two girls are sitting on top of what is left of their attempt at a sand sculpture. Thinking it would be a popular concept, they had tried to make a replica of the lighthouse. But they underestimated the weight of the sand. When their masterpiece was only half built, it collapsed in on itself. Rather than being upset, they laughed at themselves.

Realizing they didn't have enough time to create anything before the three o'clock deadline, they decided to make a throne out of it. It's working rather well in that capacity, giving them a great view of the festivities. Sam spots her mom and the twins at the far end. The two little girls are carrying huge globs of spun sugar, their faces and hands covered with it.

There are at least twenty teams working under the hot sun, with only a few minutes left to go in the contest. Sam is very impressed with John and Hunter's entry. When John asked to borrow her small wooden carving of the sea creature earlier, she should have known better. He's using it now as a guide to carving out their masterpiece.

"Where did your brother learn how to do that?" Sam asks Ally.

"Who knows? Probably some random sand castle class in Scouts," Ally adds sarcastically. "Or maybe it's a natural talent. He's good at working with clay, too. You should have seen the sculpture he did in his pottery class last year at high school. I obviously missed out on that artistic trait."

Laughing, Sam starts burying their feet in the cooler, damp sand, but then stops when she sees a familiar form standing close by. "Erica!" she exclaims, sitting up straight and shielding her eyes from the sun.

The little girl spins towards her, startled. When she sees Sam and Ally, her small mouth forms an o, and her eyes register alarm. Without a word, she takes off towards the water and quickly runs in up to her waist before being knocked down by an incoming wave.

Lunging forward, Sam is momentarily tripped up by the sand covering her feet, and she flails her arms to keep her balance. Ally has better luck and reaches Erica before Sam. Scooping her up under the arms as a wave begins to cover her blonde head, Ally hauls her out of the water just in time. Coughing and sputtering, Erica begins to cry.

"What are you doing? Get away from her!"

Startled, Ally turns and quickly sets Erica on the ground, in front of Kevin. Looking awkward in his street clothes among all of the beachgoers, he picks Erica up and scowls at both Ally and Sam. "You've been asked before not to bother my daughter," he says angrily, stepping away from them.

"We weren't bothering her!" Sam argues. "She just ran past us and out into the water. You're lucky that Ally was so quick."

Unfazed by her comment, Kevin turns to go.

"I don't wanna go with you!" Erica hollers, wiggling to get out of his grasp. "I want my mom! I want Carrie!"

Ignoring her pleas, he shushes her and stomps back through the sand, towards their house.

Looking at Ally in frustration, Sam then turns her attention to the receding ocean and the distant lighthouse.

We're coming soon, Carrie, she promises, more sure now than ever that the missing girl is real.

18

NO TURNING BACK NOW

John and Hunter take fourth place in the sand castle contest, and are proudly wearing their victory t-shirts when they meet up with the girls at the trailhead. It's a little past four and the tide is getting close to its lowest point. They got permission to go on the trail after promising to stay away from the cliff, so Sam's parents know where they're going. She's feeling a bit guilty about the obvious omission of their visit to the lighthouse, but it's necessary in order for their plan to work.

"Nice shirts," Ally laughs, holding her sides. Sam was too anxious to pay attention, but now that Ally points it out, she has to agree that they're silly. On the front is the lighthouse, a murky light shining out from the top. The back of the shirt says 'Wood's Cove Annual Sandcastle Festival, 2015' and the word, 'Winner!' in bold letters. Underneath that is a cartoonish picture of the Wood Cove Sea Monster.

"Thanks," John says, leading the way. Smoothing out the wrinkles, he then tugs at the hem of the shirt. "I think it brings out the blue in my eyes."

"At least we actually *made* a sandcastle," Hunter adds, not taking the joking as well as John.

"I thought you should have gotten third." Sam surprises her brother with the compliment, and he hesitates, unsure of how to respond. "I heard some people talking about it, and I guess that the mayor's kid made the shipwreck that won. It was good, but not as good as your monster."

They've gone a ways up the trail by now, and Hunter stops for a moment to look at his sister. "Really?" he asks, all mocking aside.

"Uh-huh," Sam confirms. "But I think the only other thing third place got that you didn't, were white ribbons."

"We don't need no stinkin' ribbons," Hunter says in his best cowboy voice, hopping over a fallen log. "We got these awesome shirts!"

They all keep up the nervous banter and senseless conversation until they reach the tree that was struck by lightning. Now that they're at the fork, their moods change and they become more serious. With silent looks of confirmation, they take the overgrown trail to the left.

Pushing through the underbrush, Ally is the last to head into the denser forest, and she watches the others with interest. She doesn't understand how they can all seem so relaxed, because she's terrified.

"You okay, Ally?" Sam is holding back a long branch to prevent it from snapping at her friend. She can see the fear on her face.

"Well…let's see," Ally states, crossing her arms over her chest. "We're in the middle of the woods, trying to find a boat that we don't even know will still float, to take out into the ocean to a secret location we might not be able to find. Once there, our goal is to figure out if there is a girl being held against her will by some big scary guys inside a falling down, haunted lighthouse. Why wouldn't I be okay?"

Sam can't stop herself from smiling. "I guess I can see your point. Want to go back?"

Ally knows that Sam means it. She would never try to make her do something she didn't want to, even if it were important to her. But it's not like they're looking for a lost dog. Ally would always wonder about the girl Carrie, and if she really existed, if they don't find out for themselves.

"And miss out on all the fun?" Ally finally answers, taking the branch from Sam's hand so she can walk past it. "Never!"

Sam's smile broadens and her pace quickens so that they can catch up with the boys. The twinge of excitement that had been brewing slowly starts to spread, giving her an extra burst of energy. She knows that they're close to solving this mystery. Now they just have to find that boat!

It isn't long before they reach a small

clearing, and on the other side, they discover the marshy cove that Captain Brown described. It's obvious by the muddy grass that there's a much larger area of water when the tide is up, but right now, they'll have to walk through the muck before getting to where it's deep enough to float a boat. However, there is no boat in sight.

"Where is it?" Sam cries desperately, her hopes fading.

"Hold on," John urges, looking around slowly. "If it's really been a few years since anyone has been here, it could be covered up. We should spread out and look along the edge, where it would be tied up."

Following his directions, they start making their way clumsily through the overgrown brush and weeds, their feet getting sucked down into the swampy ground. After ten minutes, Sam is on the verge of tears, but then Hunter suddenly whoops triumphantly!

"I found it!" he shouts, waving his arms over his head. He's on the far end of the open space, underneath some trees so that they can hardly see him. Rushing over, the four of them work together to pull the vines, weeds and debris from the old, wooden boat.

Once they're done, what's revealed isn't that impressive. "Do you think it'll float?" Sam asks John, not feeling very optimistic.

"I don't see any holes in it," John replies. "These old things can go through a lot and still be seaworthy. Come on!" he orders, grabbing an end. "Let's drag it out."

It takes several long minutes to get the boat out into the water, and Sam is beginning to worry about the time. The tide has to be all the way out by now and they won't have that long before it starts to turn back again. She can see the open ocean just beyond the trees overhanging the entrance into their small hideout, and for the first time she questions their plan. She's so distracted by the thought that she hardly notices that the boat is floating.

"It works!" Ally gasps in surprise. "I don't see any water inside of it."

"And there are even a couple of solid oars," Hunter adds, holding them up for emphasis.

"We have to go now, if we're going to do this," John states, thinking the same thing as

Sam. "We don't have much time before the tide comes in and blocks the way."

It takes some tricky maneuvering, but they manage to drag the decent sized boat out. It's big enough for four people, so they all just fit. It's a good thing both of the boys are good at rowing, because navigating is no easy task. Fortunately, they're in a protected spot, so there are just some large swells to get over, rather than breakers. It's surprising how fast they move, with the outgoing tide helping them along. In less than fifteen minutes, they're searching the coastline for the telltale triangle shaped rocks.

"There!" Sam calls out, pointing towards the impossible-to-miss rocks. Jutting up dramatically from the water, they form a perfectly sized tunnel. The old rowboat easily slips through.

Once on the other side, they find themselves in a large, protected space. It's basically a bowl made of rock, and there is only one area that they can pull the boat up on. Sam shudders at the thought of what would happen to anyone caught there during high tide.

They carefully pick their way over the wet

slippery rocks, and up the only path available to the top. Sam breaths a huge sigh of relief as she feels the fresh wind on her face when she reaches the surface. Turning, she grabs Ally's hand and helps pull her up beside her. Together, the four of them look in triumph at the lighthouse that towers over them.

"Now what?" Hunter asks, straining to see the top of the huge structure less than fifty feet away.

"Now we find out if Carrie is real, and if she's in there," Sam declares.

"I'm afraid I will have to change your plans!"

Ally cries out at the voice behind them, and all four kids spin as one to face the man standing there. Sam has never seen him before, but he has the same large build and menacing look as the other two on the boat. The one big difference is that he's holding a gun. And it's pointed right at them!

19

DEAD MAN'S POINT

"You will come with me!" the man barks, his accent very thick. Pointing at an old wooden building behind him with his free hand, he makes a sweeping gesture with the gun, guiding them towards it. The shed had been at their backs so they didn't notice it, and the man had obviously come from there. Sam could kick herself for not being more cautious, but the claustrophobia she'd been feeling in the confining rock formation had distracted her.

When the four kids don't immediately follow his command, their captor gets red in the face and takes a menacing step towards them.

"Do you not understand your situation?" he yells, waving the gun for emphasis. He mutters something in a foreign language before coming up with the words in English. "You will do as you are told. Now!" Spittle flies from his mouth and his eyes widen further, giving him a wild look. This kicks them into motion, and John is the first to move, stepping in front of Sam and Ally with his arms open wide in a protective gesture.

"Okay, okay," he says quietly, the waver in his voice the only real evidence of his fear. "We're going."

Numbly, they file inside the dark building and turn to face the man as he closes the door loudly behind them. Ally has taken hold of Sam's arm in a desperate, vice-like grip and won't let go. Although this isn't the first time they've had a gun pointed at them, that does nothing to weaken the cold claws of fear. Sam can barely breathe.

"Sit against that wall," the man orders, nodding his head towards the other side of the room. "And be quiet."

While John is nearly as tall as the older man, he's a good fifty pounds lighter and would be no match in a fight, even if there weren't a gun involved. They could probably overpower him if they all rushed him at the same time…but there *is* a gun, so they have no other choice than to do what they're told.

Sam's mind races as she settles down onto the hard wood floor. This guy doesn't know who they are. She's never seen him before, but figures he must be the fourth man that the little boy told John and Hunter about. As far as he knows, they're just some kids out snooping around, except for what he heard them say. She might still be able to talk her way out of it.

"We're really sorry for trespassing, mister!" she blurts out, allowing real tears to blur her vision.

When he turns his attention to her, Sam bravely continues. "We didn't know we weren't allowed on this property. You see, we're renting one of the beach houses, and we met a girl named Carrie that was staying next door. I guess she ran away or something, because she's been missing for a while now. We just thought she might be hiding out here so we wanted to check. We'll never come back, though," she rushes on.

She can see him hesitating and the gun lowers ever so slightly. "I promise! Our parents would kill us if they knew we were trespassing!" she grimaces at her use of the word 'kill,' but is encouraged that she has him confused.

Sam's hopes swell when the gun drops loosely at his side. He seems tempted to believe that they're just there by chance. She imagines that he would like nothing better than to get rid of them and the hassle they represent.

"There is no one here but me," he finally replies, placing a hand on the doorknob...the pathway to freedom.

"We can see that now, mister," John adds convincingly, taking Sam's lead. "We'll never come back again. We're going home in a day, anyway. We're done trying to find that girl. We'll let her parents worry about her."

Nodding his head abruptly as he makes up his mind, the man turns the knob and then opens the door a few inches, telling them to stand. But before they can, a loud crackling static emits from a large two-way radio sitting on the only table in the room.

"Regan. Regan! Check in." The man releases the door and crosses to the radio in two long steps, motioning at the same time for the kids to stay seated. Sam's hopes plummet and the dramatic dips in emotion are making her feel a bit sick to her stomach.

"Regan here. Ready for afternoon report. Switch to secondary channel." The microphone looks small in his meaty hand as he grips it tightly. Looking at the four kids, he must be trying to figure out what to say about them.

"Switching to secondary channel," the box squawks, followed by a brief pause while Regan reaches out, and turns a nob. "Go with report."

The voice on the other end has become distorted and there is more static, which is likely why this channel wouldn't be used by anyone else.

"I have some...young pirates. They were looking for treasure." Regan watches them as he says this, his expression unreadable.

"How many?" The voice has changed, and Sam looks in alarm at Ally. It's Kevin!

"Four: two boys and two girls. Claim to be

looking for a lost neighbor." Sam winces as he says this, knowing that the same story that nearly freed them will now seal their fate.

"Does one of them have red hair?" The static has gotten worse, so that his voice is almost drowned out, but the message still comes through.

"Affirmative," Regan answers with some surprise, looking at Ally with suspicion. "What are your instructions? I was going to release the…trespassers."

"Negative," Kevin replies immediately. "We'll have our order completed tonight. Those four are a liability. Repeat…they are a liability. Put them with the treasure. Rendezvous time is moved up to the next low tide at o-four hundred."

"What if someone comes looking for the….pirates?" Regan asks after a brief hesitation.

"I doubt they're there with permission," Kevin replies logically. "By the time anyone realizes it, we'll be long gone."

"Affirmative. Out." Regan drops the mic on the table and turns on the group with a new sense of purpose. "You," he says, pointing at

John. "Come here."

Ally grabs at John's hand when he stands up, but he gently shakes her off and follows Regan's order. Stopping a few feet away from the man, John crosses his arms over his chest and raises his eyebrows questioningly. Sam knows that he must be scared, but he's doing a good job at hiding it. She figures that he came to the same conclusions as she has, based on what Kevin just said. Regan wasn't told to hurt them, just to put them somewhere. Sam assumes that the 'treasure' is Carrie, and that they'll soon be joining her.

"You, too." Regan then directs Hunter, pointing to a spot next to John. Hunter isn't quite as good as John is at hiding his fear, and his legs nearly buckle when he rises, but Sam catches and steadies him. When both boys are standing in front of Regan, he keeps the gun pointed at them while rummaging through an open toolbox on the table. After a couple of minutes of searching, he smiles and brings out a bag of zip ties. Tossing it to John, he then nods at Hunter. "Tie him up."

John's cheeks burn a deep red in contrast to his blonde hair as he reluctantly secures Hunter's wrists. Regan doesn't object to him keeping his hands in front of him, but gives the plastic strips an extra tug to make sure they are tight. He then binds John's wrists in the same way, before escorting them all back outside into the bright, late afternoon sun.

Sam is a bit insulted that Regan didn't feel it was necessary to restrain her and Ally, but then nearly laughs aloud at the absurd thought. Barely containing the hysterical giggles, Sam carefully picks her way over the uneven ground and follows the others towards the lighthouse. She focuses on the hope that Regan's underestimating them will be their one advantage, but it won't do them any good if she totally loses it. Taking deep breaths, Sam gets a loose control on her raging emotions.

Ally is having a more difficult time. Crying, she turns back to look at the man trailing behind them. "Please let us go," she begs, tripping over a rock and nearly falling. Catching herself by grabbing onto Hunter, she holds onto his arm. "We promise not to tell anyone you're here!"

Regan's cold eyes study the young girl's face, no sign of remorse registering on his hard-edged features. "That is no longer an option," he says evenly. "Do as you are told and no one will be harmed."

As bleak as the situation is, his words seem to have a calming effect on Ally. She straightens her shoulders, and visibly struggles to choke back the sound of her crying. Sam quickly steps up to Ally's side and throws a steadying arm around her. Ally turns into her sideways embrace, and the two of them approach the base of the lighthouse together.

John is already standing at the large, old wooden door set into the stucco walls. He's studying them with obvious concern, his hands already turning a bit red from the ties cutting into the circulation. Sam watches his expression change to alarm when the door behind him is suddenly pulled open, and he nearly falls backwards. Standing there is the larger of the two men from the boat, Her Vaere Drager. He takes in the group gathered there, before turning on Regan.

They argue loudly in a foreign language for nearly five minutes. Sam figures it has to be Danish, and she's thankful that she has no idea what they're saying. Do all of these guys have explosive anger issues? Reminding herself not to antagonize them, she tries not to stare, and instead studies their surroundings. It might come in handy later.

The huge, hundred-foot structure is set about fifty feet back from the trail they used. The bluff angles up sharply behind it, ending in what Sam imagines must be a sheer cliff. It's clear that the only way here is by the slippery slope they climbed, in this unforgiving landscape.

"Why don't they come for us now?" The second man demands in English. It would seem that the argument is over, but he is still agitated.

"I told you, Jacque," Regan replies, throwing his one gun-free hand up. "We will be done with all of this mess by tonight. The tide will be out again at three-thirty. Take them upstairs, then secure everything, and prepare to leave."

Still muttering to himself, Jacque pulls his own pistol out from his waistband, and takes over their imprisonment. As the big door closes behind them and he yells at them to start climbing the steep, spiral staircase; Sam suddenly longs to have Regan back in charge.

The stairs go on forever. In what feels like an endless upwards, swirling trek, Sam concentrates on her grip on the loose banister and the creaking wooden steps under her feet. Captain Brown said that the lighthouse was determined to be unsafe years ago, so her fear of falling through the old stairwell to her death is probably not that far-fetched.

Just when Sam's fear starts to overwhelm her again, they come to a large platform in front of another door. The stairs continue beyond that, but Jacque calls out for them to stop. Shooing them away from the lock, he takes hold of a solid bar that disengages a new dead bolt, recently installed.

As the bolt scrapes against the wood, and Jacque pushes the large door open, Sam eagerly cranes her neck to get a look in the room. On the far side of an impressive chamber, a girl sits on the bare floor. Hugging her knees to her chest, green eyes wide with fear, she looks to be about the same age as John.

They all step into the space without any encouragement from their captor, who slams and locks the door behind them without comment.

"Carrie?" Sam calls out, her terror at their situation briefly forgotten. "We're here to help you!"

20

THE TREASURE

Carrie sits blinking at them for a moment, confused by the group that has suddenly appeared before her. Pushing herself to her feet, she is taller than Sam had imagined. Her cut-offs are covered in dirt, and the white tank top she's wearing isn't much better. She has the same unique eyes and long, thick black hair as her mother. Even though it's a tangled mess, it doesn't mask her striking beauty.

"*You're* here to rescue me?" she finally says sarcastically, after studying each of them. "Please tell me that your parents or the authorities are right behind you?"

Well, she definitely has her mom's personality, too, Sam thinks, her excitement at finding the girl quickly fading.

When they all silently exchange knowing looks, Carrie sighs loudly. "Oh, this is just *great!*" Kicking at an empty can on the floor, she stomps over to a dirty mattress with a lone sheet and plops down on it. "Who are you?" she demands, holding her head in her hands in a defeated gesture.

"Well, you're welcome," Hunter blurts back, his tone matching hers. "It's not like we didn't risk our lives or anything to get out here and find you." He holds his bound hands out in front of him for emphasis. "Do you think we're having *fun?*"

Blinking again, Carrie lowers her hands and places them loosely in her lap. Sam suddenly realizes that the poor girl is probably in shock. She's been locked up in here for at least a week. Quickly crossing the room, she kneels down next to her so that they're at eye level.

"Carrie, my name is Samantha Wolf. That's my brother, Hunter. This is my best friend, Allyson Parker," Sam continues, pointing to Ally, "and her brother, John. We rented the beach house next to yours, at Wood Cove. It's a long story, but after meeting your little sister, mom, and dad, we got a bit suspicious."

"Wait. My *dad?*" Carrie interrupts, her pretty face contorting in anger.

"Kevin," Ally answers, coming to sit on the other side of the lumpy mattress.

"Kevin is *not* my dad!" she nearly yells, hands balling up into fists. "Is Erica okay?" she asks before anyone can respond, turning quickly to Sam with a concerned expression.

Her rapid change in demeanor makes her hard to follow, and Sam shakes her head briefly to try to think clearly. "Erica and your mom seem to be okay, Carrie," she says calmly, her eyes flitting to Ally, hoping that her friend understands how fragile she really is. "We suspected that Kevin wasn't who he said he was, and we uncovered some things that were pretty strange. When we saw your S.O.S. flashing last night, we decided to come find out if you were really here or not, but..." she looks sheepishly at her brother and John. "Things didn't really go quite the way we had planned. We're sorry we aren't more help to you, but we promise we'll find a way out of here!"

As both Sam and Ally place a reassuring hand on her cold, dirty arms, the young girl finally breaks out in silent, wracking sobs. Scooting up next to her, Sam puts an arm around her waist and motions to the concerned boys to just let her cry. After a good ten minutes, Carrie finally takes a big shuddering breath and smiles weakly at them.

"I'm sorry," she whispers, wiping at her running nose. "I've just been so scared. I didn't think anyone was ever going to come."

"You don't need to apologize." Ally is quick to reassure her. "I can't imagine what it's been like for you!"

"Carrie," John says gently, leaning against a nearby support beam. "Do you mind if I ask *why* you're here? We figured out some stuff, but we really don't know what's going on."

"How much do you know?" Carrie asks, already looking stronger.

John describes everything that has happened since they arrived at Wood's Cove, with the rest of them adding to the story as necessary. Sam is rewarded with an approving smile when she explains how she made the connection to her cell phone cover on the boat, and Erica's missing sister.

"I'm impressed," Carrie admits, when John finishes with his deciphering the S.O.S. signal she sent the night before. "But there's a whole lot you *don't* know," she continues, the smile vanishing. "My mom is in a lot of trouble."

"What kind of trouble?" Hunter mumbles around the zip tie that he's trying to bite through. They're the thick ones and all he's accomplished so far are some sore teeth. "And how'd you know how to make that distress signal?"

"I was in Scouts," she answers the simple question first. "Jacque forgot the lantern again last night, so I got a couple of series off before he remembered and came up."

Sam once again finds herself wishing she had joined Ally's aunt's troop when she'd invited them a couple of years ago. Then she realizes what Carrie's explanation means. "They leave you alone up here all night without even a light?" she asks, looking at the teen with a new respect.

"I get the lantern until it's dark enough for it to show from a distance." She shrugs, as if it's no big deal. "But forget about the light. I need to explain about BioCore, and then we need to figure out a way to escape."

"Why?" Hunter questions, having given up on chewing his way to freedom. "According to what Kevin just said over the radio, they're gonna be done tonight with whatever it is they're doing. It sounded like they're picking up those two guys down there at low tide and getting out of here. Why cause problems? We just have to wait until our parents figure out where we are...and they will. They're good at that."

"No!" Carrie is shaking her head impatiently. "You don't understand! They'll *never* let my mom go. They can't! They won't let me or Erica go, either. I'm sure they'll leave the four of *you* up here, but not me." Standing up, she begins to pace the room.

"Doesn't your mom work for them?" Ally wonders. "Why are they doing this to her?"

"My mom is a scientist," Carrie explains. "A geneticist. She has her own small development company. Several years ago, she came up with something that is going to change the world of medicine. A way to genetically alter a virus, and then use that to fight illnesses. Her only problem was that it was theoretical. She didn't have the facilities or specialized equipment to create it. That's where BioCore came in."

Already tired from her few trips across the room, Carrie sits back down in between Sam and Ally.

"Mom had gone to just about everyone she could think of, pitching her idea and trying to get the funding she needed. After a year, she was ready to give up. Her company was struggling by then because of all the time she was spending on it, instead of the paying jobs the rest of her employees were trying to get done. But then Kevin showed up. It was like a dream come true. They offered her a grant large enough to rent out the lab and everything else she needed."

"Didn't she know about the shady stuff they did?" John interrupts, hoping he wasn't going to offend her.

"If you're talking about what happened over in Africa," Carrie states, turning her flashing green eyes on John. "That wasn't reported until just this past year, long after Mom started working for them three years ago. I don't remember all that much from then, but I do know that at the time, they were only involved in government contracts. At least, that's all that was publicized. They seemed legit, and Mom was convinced that it was the answer to her prayers. At first...it was. Everything was going great for the first time since my dad died when I was ten. We moved into a huge house so that we could be closer to the lab. Mom was able to hire a special team from her own company to assist her. It was slow, tedious work, but she was always very positive and happy. That is, until a few months ago."

"What happened?" Sam prompts when Carrie falls silent, lost in her thoughts.

"The article you read was brought to her attention, and after she started asking questions about it, her team began acting strange around her. Kevin gave her a bunch of excuses, but my mom is smart. Like a literal genius. She wasn't falling for it and I could tell she was nervous and having second thoughts about the whole program. But...she was *so* close to being able to apply for a patent and start patient trials. That's when it happened.

"I'll never forget the look on her face when she came home that night," Carrie says quietly, her voice going hoarse with emotion. "It was a couple of weeks ago. Mom was getting ready to turn in her final work to BioCore, and file it with the US patent office at the same time. To celebrate, she rented the beach house for a whole two months. We've come every year since I can remember, but we usually only stay for a week. We were all really looking forward to spending the whole summer here and taking some time together before she got even busier.

"But something had gone horribly wrong. What was supposed to be a congratulations dinner at work turned into an ambush. Kevin had already gotten to the three other scientists working for Mom and bought them out."

"Bought them out?" Sam repeats, growing more confused. "I don't understand. Wasn't he already paying them?"

"No. BioCore gave my mom several million dollars in grant money, and she in turn used that to pay her employees. They were still technically working for her company. The agreement was that BioCore gets their name attached to the patent, as well as my mom, which is basically the power to control how the invention is used. But BioCore has other plans. They never intended to file it, because they don't want to use the technology to create just medicine. They want to secretly make the medicine and sell it to the highest bidder, and…" Carrie wrings her hands nervously, looking back up at her now captive audience. "And they're going to force my mom to use the same methods to turn it into a biological weapon!"

Sam has watched enough movies and read enough books to know what Carrie is talking about, but it's still difficult to believe it. It was hard to accept that someone would actually be capable of taking something meant for saving lives, and turn it into a way to harm people.

"I still don't understand how they can *make* your mom do that," Sam finally breaks the stunned silence that has settled over the room. "Why didn't she just go to the police or something?"

"And tell them what?" Carrie retorts,

clearly frustrated. "It's called corporate espionage, and she *did* try to go to the FBI. But like I said, BioCore had already paid off her team and gotten them to agree to it. For months, they had been working to frame my mom, and make it look like *she* was the one plotting all of it. So by the time she found out, it was too late. Kevin basically told her to either work with them, or end up in a federal prison for the rest of her life. She pretended to go along with it, but we left in the middle of the night and came out here. The next day she tried to arrange a meeting with the FBI. But...Kevin showed up instead. She really underestimated them. While she was gone, those goons downstairs kidnapped me and brought me here."

"This doesn't make any sense," Hunter interrupts. "If they're so rich and powerful, why didn't they just lock you all up at their company until your mom did what they wanted?"

"He has a point," John agrees. "I don't understand why they would bother with this whole charade. They knew where your mom was and that she tried to report them to the FBI. Why take a chance of her telling someone by leaving her and Erica at the beach house? There had to be a better place to keep you then here!"

"Oh my gosh," Carrie huffs, frustrated. "I *told* you, she was still a week away from finishing. She had to have access to her lab, the equipment, files, and virus samples. It took about two years to build that stuff and it's the only lab of its kind in the whole country. Only a few places in the world are set up for the kind of virus work she's doing. They couldn't just 'lock her in a room' until everything was done.

"She's also well known in her field and very active in several scientific groups. If she suddenly disappeared when she was about to achieve her life's work...the feds would have swarmed her lab and locked everything down. So they had no choice but to keep her out in the open and let her go to the lab. It's a two-hour drive from here, and the other scientists that betrayed her are there, watching everything she does. But they had to have a sure way to control her, which is why they took me.

"They didn't expect her to run, so they had to improvise when she came to the beach house. At first, they had me on their boat, but after I nearly escaped a second time, they brought me out here.

"For the past two weeks, they've been coercing Mom into finishing the rest of the work so that they can move forward with the human trials in a country where no one will even know what they're doing. Don't you see?" Carrie cries, looking to John because he is the oldest. "She didn't have a choice but to go along with it. But I know my mom, and she'll *never* help them develop it into a weapon. We *have* to get out of here before they come back! The only way to prove all of this is for Kevin to be caught while he's here with mom and the incriminating documents are in his possession. Otherwise, they'll never let us go!"

"Well then, we better get to work."

Carrie looks at Sam in surprise. Still sitting beside her, Sam has found a tear in the bottom edge of the mattress and has part of a metal spring pulled out of the hole. "And I know how we're going to escape!"

21

GOT A LADDER?

The spring breaks free from the mattress as Sam makes her bold claim, and she looks up triumphantly with the prize in her hand. Everyone except John looks confused, and he eagerly comes to sit in front of Sam, holding his bound wrists out a little further.

"Good thinking, Sam!" he says approvingly, causing her to blush slightly.

Concentrating on scraping the plastic with the jagged end of metal, she's careful not to cut into his wrists. This is going to take a while. "I've been looking at the windows," she says, without looking up. "There's no way any of us could fit through the two small ones, but that old stained-glass one up high might work."

The two square windows are set low to the ground and face the cove, but there's a large round opening near the tall ceiling, overlooking the sea. Sam figures it had ornate stained glass it at one point, based on the remnants clinging to the edges and the colored fragments littering the floor below it.

Carrie is straining to get a good look at it, but then slowly shakes her head. "I don't know, Sam," she says, standing and going to the wall below it. "We're about seventy feet off the ground here. I think this used to be the room the light keeper would stay in. The actual spotlight is above us. Jacque took me up there once, to give me some fresh air. They stopped letting me out to bathe after I took off down the beach one time," she adds quietly.

"Is there a balcony or anything up there?" Hunter asks, suddenly interested in the plan. "It looks like there's a big widow's walk around the whole thing in this picture," he explains, pointing at the lighthouse on the front of his shirt. Ally grabs at his t-shirt and pulls the material tight, so she can see the picture more clearly.

"Yeah, there is," Carrie confirms. "But I didn't dare go out on it, even if Jacque would have let me. Who knows if it'll hold up under any weight? This whole thing is falling apart!"

"Well, that might be our best chance," Sam tells her. "Or our *only* chance. There!" she shouts, as John gives his hands an extra tug and the weakened plastic snaps in half. "Next?" she says, turning to Hunter, who is already stepping up eagerly.

After what seems much longer than it really is, due to Hunter's impatience, they're all gathered below the window. It's a good four feet above John's head, but Sam figures she can reach it by standing on his shoulders. John fastened the bedsheet around her waist, and then added Ally's long swimsuit cover-up she was wearing, and his and Hunter's t-shirts to try to make it long enough. Sam could almost laugh at the irony, looking at the distorted lighthouse and Sea Creature dangling at the end.

"What if the balcony isn't right above that window?" Ally is bouncing back and forth on her feet anxiously. The whole idea of Sam climbing out a window over seventy feet off the ground is terrifying. "Or what if it collapses?"

"We'll catch her," John tries to reassure his sister. "If this make-shift rope isn't long enough, then she isn't going to even try to reach it. Right, Sam?"

"Right," Sam confirms, taking a few deep breaths to calm her shaking legs. "Let's do this."

John kneels down so that Sam can step cautiously onto his shoulders, with Ally and Hunter on either side to help her. She wobbles precariously as he stands slowly, and reaches out to put a hand against the cold stone wall for stability. She's able to grab at the windowsill before he's even all the way up, taking some of the weight off his shoulders. "I got it!" she calls triumphantly, careful not to put her hands over any sharp pieces of glass.

Once John is standing, she's high enough that she can easily pull herself up into the window, balancing in the opening, the thick stucco wall providing a wide ledge. Trying hard not to look down at the dizzying ground below, Sam instead looks up, and is relieved to see the underside of the walkway less than two feet above her. "I can reach it!" she calls back into the room. Looking down at her friends, she finds that Hunter is now sitting on John's shoulders, holding tightly to the end of her rope. This will give her the extra few feet that she needs.

Bracing her hands on either side of the open circle, she squats inside the window and then slowly stands, leaning out slightly so that she can grab onto one of the balcony's braces with both hands. Having accomplished this, Sam feels a sudden rush of fear, realizing the dangerous position she's now in, leaning out and away from the window. The bedsheet is pulling tightly at her waist and she knows there isn't any more slack.

"Sam!" John calls urgently. "What are you doing? Can you make it?"

"Come back, Sam!" Ally pleads, her voice full of dread.

Looking around desperately, Sam tries to find a way to go up, since she isn't sure that she can make it back without falling. The balcony is made of wrought iron bars, spaced evenly apart. There are several spots where the metal has become corroded and fallen away, and fortunately, one of these areas is just to the right of the brace Sam is clinging to. Still holding onto it tightly, she shuffles her feet over until she is under the hole. Nearly crying now, Sam forces herself to let go with one hand and reach up into the hole, grasping the nearest bar. When it doesn't come loose, she gives it a little tug and it feels secure. Her confidence growing slightly, she does the same with her other hand. When she stands to her full height, her head and shoulders fit through the hole and she's able to lift herself up the rest of the way.

Rolling over onto the balcony, she ends up face down, which is a big mistake. The craggy cliffs, buffeted by large waves crashing against them, appear tiny below her. There's no question that one wrong move would mean the end of her. Temporarily frozen with fear, she might have stayed there forever, if it weren't for Ally frantically calling her name. Someone is also tugging slightly at the sheet around her waist.

Starting with her left foot, she carefully slides it over until it's inside the lighthouse. The windows lining the balcony were broken out long ago, so there is nothing standing in her way. Still too afraid to speak, she goes through the same motions with her left hand, and closes her eyes in relief when she gets a firm grip on the inside ledge. Using what strength she has left, she pulls herself across the bars and then finally falls to the safety of the floor.

The tension on the sheet goes limp, followed by a cry of terror from Ally. Sam quickly hops up onto her knees and calls out to her friend. "I'm okay!" she shouts, hopefully loud enough for them to hear her, but no one else. "I made it!"

Encouraged by the following cheers and clapping, Sam sits back against the wall in relief. She needs to take a minute to pull herself together, and isn't sure if her legs will hold her weight.

After what feels like too much time, she takes one more deep breath and gingerly stands, while looking around the new, round room. It's very big, with a huge lamp fixed in the middle of it. There's no light bulb in it, and it probably hasn't worked for a long time, but Sam can imagine how bright it must have been. Happy to see that she's alone, she quickly locates the door and tiptoes down the stairs, cringing at the creaking that can't be avoided.

Breathing much easier once she reaches the landing and the bolted door, it takes her a few tense minutes to work the large bar loose. She's finally rewarded with four huge grins waiting for her on the other side of the door. Ally is the first to gather her up in a big hug.

"I thought you fell!" she gasps, trying hard not to start crying again.

"Sorry," Sam whispers, barely able to breath inside the tight embrace. "I was too scared to talk!" Pushing back gently from her friend, she looks anxiously over her shoulder, towards the descending stairwell. They're a long ways from being free.

"We still have over four hours before the tide will be low enough for us to leave," John explains, looking in the same direction.

"So we don't wait," Hunter says matter-of-factly. "Let's just make a run for the trail and get as far away from here as we can!" Sam is tempted to agree with him, but Carrie is shaking her head.

"The first day they brought me here, I ran off as soon as I stepped on solid ground," she tells Hunter. "I knew about the trail from the other times we came to the Cove. But it only goes for a couple-hundred feet on this end, before being totally blocked by rocks on one side, and a cliff on the other. I don't think there's anywhere on this point that we could hide without being found right away. They pretty much laughed at me when I tried."

"What's their routine?" John asks, choosing a different tactic.

"Well, I already had dinner. Jacque should be back up soon, since it's getting dark. I usually hand the lantern out to him, and he goes away without even saying anything. He's a man of few words. If I need to use the bathroom, I let him know. There's an old outhouse in the back."

"Where does he go after he takes the lantern?" Ally asks.

"He goes out to the shack. That's where they sleep."

"So then I need to go hide back upstairs," Sam decides. "It'll be dark in here anyway, with just the one small lantern, so I doubt he'll even notice that I'm gone. Here, take the sheet," she continues, untying it from her waist. "Bunch the shirts up under it to make it look like I'm lying on the mattress. After he leaves, I'll come back down and let you out."

Everyone agrees that it's the best option they have, so Sam locks them back inside after another round of hugs. Once she returns to the light room, though, her restored bravery falters. With the sun quickly setting on the distant horizon, the shadows are already becoming thick around her. Trying hard not to think of the ghost story, she sits down behind an overturned table and hugs her knees tightly to her chest.

22

PIRATES AND A SEA MONSTER

Sam can't be sure how long she's been hiding, but nearly half an hour has passed since she heard Jacques finally come up the stairs for the lantern, and then go back down. There were several tense minutes while she waited to see if the footsteps would continue up to where she was, but he obviously didn't notice she was gone from the other shadowy room.

It's so dark now, that she can barely see her hand in front of her face. The constant feeling that someone is about to grab her back is driving her crazy. Sam has never really been afraid of the dark, but she's pretty sure that from now on, she'll want to sleep with a nightlight.

Crawling on her hands and knees, Sam peeks over the edge of what used to be windows, and confirms that there's a very faint light glowing far below, reassuring her that Jacques and Regan are in the shed, not the lighthouse. Beyond the point, she can see small flickers of a different kind of light on the distant beach. Guilt momentarily replaces her fear, because she knows that it's probably people out searching for them. She would give anything right now for a flare! But with no electricity, flashlight, or anything else to signal with, there's nothing she can do. Unfortunately, while it looks like there are boats in the cove, there aren't any coming their way. Stealing herself to move blindly through the dark, Sam takes a deep breath, scurries over to the door, and then feels her way out onto the stairs.

Scooting down the stairwell on her bottom, the way she used to as a child, Sam then stumbles across the familiar platform. When her hand closes over the cold steel of the latch, she feels an immense sense of triumph.

"It's me!" she whispers into the room, when no one is waiting for her like before. In the couple of seconds of silence before John answers her, Sam imagines all the horrible possible reasons for an empty room.

"Stay there, Sam," he orders.

Sam can just make out their shapes in the inky blackness as they move towards her. Hunter grunts as he trips over something, and Ally's giggle lightens the mood.

Sam quickly fills them in on what she saw from the lookout. "Do you think they might come looking for us here before we can get the rowboat out?" she wonders aloud, while getting a firm grip on the bannister.

John is in front of her, leading the way, and Ally is literally clinging to her back. Hunter and then Carrie bring up the rear.

"Why would they?" Carrie asks. "You told your parents that you were going on the trail. They'll be searching those woods for hours before even thinking of this lighthouse. The sheriff knows there's only one way on and off, during low tide. They have no reason to think that you're here, do they?"

"No," Sam confirms, feeling even worse for withholding the whole truth from her mom and dad. "They know I was interested in it, but like you said…it'll take a long time to get through the woods. I bet they think we've fallen off a cliff or been swept away by another landslide."

Sam tries hard to keep the emotion out of her voice, but has to swallow around a rising lump. She suddenly wishes that her dad were here. He would wrap her up in his protective strong arms and make everything okay again.

The group falls silent, as they get closer to the bottom of the lighthouse, with no way of being certain that one of the men isn't still standing guard there. Thankfully, they find the space empty and thin moonlight is shining weakly through the large, empty windows lining the walls.

"Now what?" Hunter asks John, his face looking a ghostly shade in the moon glow.

"We've got to get to the rocks," he answers quickly, looking at the moon with apprehension. Right now, darkness is the best thing they have going for them.

"We can circle around the back of the

lighthouse, and then follow the tree line instead of just running across the open space," Carrie suggests. "They'll be much less likely to spot us that way." She leads the way outside without waiting for anyone to answer, and they all trail after her without a sound.

It doesn't take long to pick their way through the low bushes and dry grass, its growth stunted by the constant wind sweeping across the point. Once they make it to the trees, they all relax a little and begin whispering to each other again.

"How late do you think it is?" Sam asks no one in particular.

"It's got to be a little after midnight by now," John answers. "So we're still going to have to wait for the tide to go out more before we can leave."

The wooden shack is now a hundred feet or so to their left and the ground suddenly falls away to reveal the steep, rocky trail. Encouraged, they scramble down, careful not to kick any of the rocks loose on the way. They have to stop short of the bottom because there is cold seawater in the way.

"There's the boat!" Hunter whispers, pointing to the far side of the enclosure. When he starts to enter the water to retrieve it, Carrie grabs at him and yanks him back.

"Are you stupid?" she nearly shouts, her eyes sparkling in the dim light making its way down to them. "The currents in there are crazy. You can't see it, but each time a wave comes in and out, the water is sucked through the opening that's still below the surface. We have to wait."

"Okay!" Hunter retorts, pulling his arm out of her grasp. "I get it! But if we wait too long, then Kevin and his goons will get here first."

No one has a reply to that, as they all consider the impossible situation that they're in. After several minutes, John is the first one to find a rock to sit on. With no other options, Sam and Ally join him to wait. Hunter is too stubborn though, so he continues to pace along the edge of the water, watching the boat. Carrie eventually joins him and they talk to each other in hushed tones.

Even though it feels like forever, Sam knows that in reality, it takes about two hours for the water to retreat enough to reveal the tunnel.

At first, she thinks it's just her eyes playing tricks on her, but then John sees it, too.

"Finally!" he expels, slapping his thighs as he stands. "We've got to get the rowboat now," he continues, taking his shirt off. He and Hunter had put the t-shirts back on at some point. "If we wait too long, it might go through the opening without us!"

Cautiously, he and Hunter enter the water. Although it only comes up to their waists now, the strong currents Carrie warned about tug at their legs, making the short walk to the boat treacherous.

When they finally secure it, the girls all quietly cheer, relieved to be another step closer to freedom. Sam notes that the tunnel is now halfway uncovered, almost enough to slip through. A sense of danger replaces her optimism at the realization that this also means Kevin could be waiting on the other side to come in.

"We have to go!" she urges, the first to climb over the side of the weathered boat. "Let's at least get to the tunnel so that we can go through as soon as it's low enough," she pushes, when Carrie and Ally hesitate.

When all five of them pile in, they end up sitting rather low in the water. It was pretty much at its limit on their way over and no one had given much thought about an extra person on the trip back.

"Are we going to sink?" Ally worries. Splashing at the water just a few inches below the rim, she looks to her brother for reassurance.

"We'll be okay so long as we aren't hit by any big waves," he answers, not exactly putting her fears at ease. "We never should have done this without the proper life jackets in the boat," he chides. "I know better than that."

Sam was right. By the time they reach the passageway, they're able to slip inside. Ducking as low as they can, they use their hands to push their way through, water dripping on them from the rocks just inches above their heads.

When they finally emerge out the other side, it takes a moment for the victory to sink in.

"We made it!" Sam is the first to shout, looking back at Dead Man's Point in disbelief. While the others join her in celebrating, Sam's eye is drawn to the top of the lighthouse.

It can't be! She thinks, rubbing at her face. But no, the light is there. Not like the white light, that's still glowing from the shack, but the faint flickering of a candle! Spinning back to tell the others, Sam looks out at the ocean for the first time since descending down into the cavern. A thick fog is rolling into the cove, and it's rapidly making its way towards them.

"Row!" John shouts to Hunter. "We could end up going in circles if we get caught in that fog!"

The boys dig at the water with all their strength, but the overloaded boat is slow to respond. Without really thinking about it, Sam kicks off her sandals and then slips out the back and into the cold water. The boat rises slightly, and she hangs onto the edge while kicking with her legs as hard as she can. It's not much, but the added buoyancy along with the forward motion is enough to help get them moving.

Just when Sam thinks they're making some progress, the sound of a motor erupts from behind them! Turning to look, she can see the vague outline of a dinghy not far away, at the edge of the wall of fog.

"That's the cruiser that Kevin uses to go back and forth from his boat!" Carrie confirms, her voice tight.

"Maybe they haven't seen us," Hunter whispers. He and John stop rowing, and the ensuing silence seems intensified by the mist still quickly approaching. Sam also stops kicking; hoping that if they just stay still and quiet, they won't be spotted.

Suddenly, a bright spotlight flashes on, illuminating the water around them before coming to rest on their upturned faces. The motor responds by revving louder, and they know that there's no way they can outrun them.

"We have to try!" Sam shouts, kicking furiously again.

John and Hunter row faster than they ever thought they could, the years of being on various outings together paying off. Ally and Carrie lean out on opposite sides, paddling with their hands. Sam can't help but to look back over her shoulder, and sees that the fog has overtaken the dinghy, it's light now creating an eerie halo.

As their adversaries race towards them, a new sound erupts to fill the night. Somewhere between the wail of a crying woman and the haunting song of a whale, it's like nothing Sam has ever heard before. The purr of the motor is drowned out by it as the fog seems to echo the call over and over again.

The hairs rising on the back of her neck, Sam stops swimming and desperately tries to pull herself from the water. But her arms are already tired, and she lacks the strength to haul herself out. Slipping back into the murky ocean, Sam feels something huge brush past her legs, just below the surface. Afraid to move, she watches in horror as the water begins to swell behind her, speeding towards the dinghy.

Strong hands grab at her from behind as the wail increases, and Sam is pulled over the side of the boat as the swell grows into a huge wave that slams into the other racing vessel. There's a moment of chaos as the dinghy is launched into the air, its motor screaming, and men shouting. It comes down on its side with a horrendous crash, and the light is extinguished before silence settles over the water.

Stunned, the five friends huddle together in the rowboat, unsure of what just happened.

The air cooled rapidly with the arrival of the fog as well as a distinct smell unique to the ocean. But Sam realizes that the mist is already thinning out when the goosebumps on her arms are soothed by the returning heat, left in the wake of the odd encounter.

When the men from the capsized boat start to call out to one another, the kids are forced back into motion. Taking up the oars, John and Hunter begin rowing again, laughing nervously about their good luck. But Sam knows that it *wasn't* luck that saved them.

"Thank you, Captain Wood!" Sam shouts into the night, as they head for the distant lights on the beach. Lights that represent their safety…and their triumph.

23

A NEW TALE TO TELL

Warm blankets and hot chocolate go a long ways towards making things better. At least, that's what Sam is thinking while staring into the steam that's rising from the mug she's holding firmly in her hands. It reminds her of the fog, and this causes her heart rate to accelerate again.

"Sam!" Jerking her head around, she looks sheepishly at her father. "The officer asked you a question. Can you describe the color of the boat?"

Sam's head is swimming from the interrogation they've been enduring for the past two hours. She's quite certain that she already answered that question twice already. She's about to tell the sheriff a third time, when his radio squawks and he puts up a hand to stop her. After several minutes of scratchy conversation, he smiles at everyone.

"The Coast Guard located them!" he announces, looking around the large family room of the beach house that's nearly full of people. "It's just how the kids told it. Lisa and Erica were locked below deck, but unhurt," he continues, nodding towards Carrie, who starts to cry from relief. "If the documents they found are really what you kids say they are, then those men will be facing some pretty stiff penalties, in addition to kidnapping and false imprisonment. The FBI and Homeland Security should be here in the morning," he adds, sounding a bit overwhelmed.

Sam's mom puts a hand on her shoulder, the reminder of how serious the situation was likely sinking in. Karen and Ethan were both understandably furious when the kids were first pulled from the water, but as the story unfolded, the anger turned to relief that everyone was okay.

Her parents had started going door-to-door at seven, when dinner passed and they were still gone. At ten, they contacted the sheriff and a search of the woods was organized. When Captain Brown got wind of what "all the fuss in the cove" was about, he quickly made his way to the beach house. He arrived not long before the fog started to form, so that everyone was already out of the woods and arranging for a boat to take them to Dead Man's Point by the time they rowed ashore.

Now, Captain Brown is leaning against the kitchen counter, the ever-present pipe hanging from his mouth. A grin has been stuck on his face since Sam's telling of their nearly disastrous capture during the escape.

No one else believed them. The sheriff referred to the 'unexplained event' as a rogue wave. He even wrote that out on the witness statement that Sam and the others each signed.

"What about Regan and Jacques?" John asks the sheriff. He's been unusually quiet this whole time, and Sam suspects it's because he's embarrassed. He's sure to feel that he let her parents down, but she plans on making it clear to them how important a role he played in keeping them all safe.

"They've been arrested," the officer replies. "They didn't go easily though, and it nearly came to gunfire. But when the Coast Guard arrived to back up my men, they realized they were outnumbered. Turns out they're criminals, but not stupid."

Hunter laughs at this, and he and John high-five each other. In spite of everything that's happened, the four of them are much closer than ever before. Sam can't imagine how things would have turned out if John and Hunter hadn't been there this time to help.

Ally has been sitting silently beside her, snuggled in a huge blanket, but now she throws it off to free her arms. Apparently having the same thoughts, she wraps Sam up in a huge embrace, then motions for their brothers and Carrie to join them.

The five of them barely fit on the oversized couch, but it doesn't matter. They make it work. With the sun just starting to break over the horizon, the room around them takes on a warm glow, matching their moods.

Over Ally's shoulder, Sam sees old Captain

Brown tip her a salute with his pipe, his grizzled face looking younger from the smile it still possesses.

Although no one else will admit to believing that the Wood's Sea Creature saved them, Sam is certain that from now on, there will be a new ending to the tale that Captain Brown tells. One that involves pirates, a treasure, a protective sea creature…and plenty of mystery!

THE END

Thank you for reading, 'The Beach House Mystery'! I hope that you enjoyed it, and will take the time to write a simple review on Amazon!

Be sure to read all of the crazy adventures Sam and Ally go on together in the 'Samantha Wolf Mysteries'!

ABOUT THE AUTHOR

Author Tara Ellis lives in a small town in beautiful Washington State, in the Pacific Northwest. She enjoys the quiet lifestyle with her two teenage kids, and several dogs. Tara was a firefighter/EMT, and worked in the medical field for many years. She now teaches CPR, and concentrates on family, photography, and writing middle grade and young adult novels.

Visit her author page on Amazon to find all of her books!

http://www.amazon.com/author/taraellis

Made in the USA
Lexington, KY
09 May 2017